W9-BSN-028

IKENGA

IKENGA

NNEDI OKORAFOR

Viking

VIKING

An imprint of Penguin Random House LLC, New York

First published in the United States of America by Viking,
an imprint of Penguin Random House LLC, 2020

Visit us online at penguinrandomhouse.com

LIBRARY OF CONGRESS CATALOGING-IN-PUBLICATION DATA IS AVAILABLE

Printed in the USA

ISBN 9780593113523

10   9   8   7   6   5   4   3   2   1

Set in LTC Kennerley   Book design by Jim Hoover

"Don't make me angry. You wouldn't
like me when I'm angry."

—David Banner from
The Incredible Hulk television series

1

A Sad Farewell with Pepper

NNAMDI DIDN'T WANT to look at his father's body in the casket, so he looked at the side of his mother's face instead. He sat beside her, his relatives all around him. He wanted to hold his mother's hand, but he didn't dare. Her black head wrap was perched on her head, all sharp starched angles. Auntie Ugochi, his mother's sister, had helped her put it on. If it weren't for Auntie Ugochi, his mother would have stayed in bed, sobbing.

Nnamdi's eyes fell on his mother's gold earrings. She only wore these on special occasions. Nnamdi figured the burial of his father was special enough. He stared at his mother now and she didn't notice. Her face was a terrible mess. Her dark brown eyes were red and puffy, her black mascara was running down her cheeks, and her nose was wet with tears and snot. The handkerchief someone had given her was soaked through with tears.

"My husband. *Ewo, ewo, ewo,*" she kept whispering as she gazed at the body of Nnamdi's father. He was yards away, lying in an open ebony casket under the black tent next to the high-reaching palm tree that grew beside the house. He was dressed in his impeccable police chief uniform, the same type of uniform he'd been wearing on the night he died. Except this one didn't have three holes in the chest and back. The murder of Nnamdi's father exactly two weeks ago was still unsolved.

The sun was especially harsh today, and even under the tent, it was sweltering hot. The humid heat blew as a wave of grief pressed down on Nnamdi's shoulders. He ran his hand over his freshly trimmed rough hair and turned from his mother to look somewhere else. For a while, he watched the women with the drums perform their burial dance before him. They wore matching blue dresses and cowry shells that clicked on their ankles. As they danced, they kicked up dust. The band had a guitar and bass player, a flutist, and three more drummers, and they played a variety of songs from highlife to traditional. Normally, Nnamdi would have enjoyed the music.

Suddenly, all the dancers missed their rhythm. The drummers lost their beat. The guitarist's fingers slipped. And the flutists missed their notes. All Nnamdi's relatives, family, friends, acquaintances—the two hundred people sitting on benches, standing, and crying in the large spacious compound—all looked toward the entranceway on the left side. Auntie Ugochi leaned toward his mother's ear and Nnamdi heard her mutter, "This man has no shame."

His mother snatched Nnamdi's hand and squeezed hard. "Keep playing, keep dancing!" she barked at the musicians and dancers. A drummer beat out a floundering rhythm and the dancers moved distractedly.

Nnamdi didn't want to look. He knew who he'd see. "Never shy away from conflict," his father had once told him. "Look it in the eye and deal with it." And his mother had stood behind his father and added, "Courage, my son. Your father means you should have courage but be *smart* about it."

So Nnamdi turned to look. He saw a procession of ten fashionably dressed, gold- and diamond-wearing, attention-usurping women and men filing into the compound. Nnamdi tried to stand up straight with his chin up, as his father would have. But instead, fear made him slump in his seat and barely lift his head.

Nnamdi remembered his father angrily talking about these individuals. "Everyone knows who they are, but people are too afraid to confront them. If anything, people treat them like Nollywood movie stars." These were the most prominent criminals in Kaleria.

That regal old woman wearing the red *abada* textile clothing had to be Mama Go-Slow. His father was right: indeed, she did "walk like a buffalo," and her expensive outfit was thrown off balance by her signature wide, blocky black shoes. The man in the suit that was too big for his skinny frame must be Never Die, the thief who had been shot by police many times but remained alive. Nnamdi was also sure he spotted Bad Market and Three Days' Journey, too. All of them were strutting like celebrities on the red carpet, when they were actually unwanted guests at the chief of police's burial service.

Leading this procession was an expensively dressed man who was even shorter than Nnamdi. Nnamdi's stomach dropped and his hands grew cold. The man looked more like a movie star than any of the others. He was handsome and carried himself like he expected the world to bow at his feet.

This was the very man most, including Nnamdi, believed was responsible for his father's murder: the Chief of Chiefs. If he hadn't been the one to pull the trigger, he'd certainly paid and ordered someone to do it. The problem was there was no proof, no gun registration, no witnesses, no confessions, nothing. It was as if a ghost had shot his father and then fled back to the spirit world to laugh about it.

But truth outshone evidence and Nnamdi knew. Everyone knew. And though he'd never seen the Chief of Chiefs with his own eyes, he was sure this was him right now. Waltzing into his father's funeral with the confidence of a ghost. Nnamdi pressed against his mother as she squeezed his hand harder. The Chief of Chiefs was the smallest grown man Nnamdi had ever seen, but he knew that this guy was the biggest crime lord in all of Kaleria, maybe even in all of Southeastern Nigeria. Kaleria was a small suburb of Owerri, so this didn't make the Chief of Chiefs anywhere as infamous as the greatest crime lords in the mega-city of Lagos. However, the Chief of Chiefs certainly dined with and had the ear of those big Lagos men.

There were so many crazy rumors about the guy. Some said that he owned huge homes on every continent, all bought with his dirty money. That he was so filthy rich that he bathed with soap made from crushed pink diamonds. That he was so successful in his criminal activity because he was the descendant of a demon and Mami Wata, the water goddess. And that at night he slept with earplugs in his ears because the sound of the stars twinkling kept him up. Nnamdi didn't believe any of this, but that didn't make the man any less creepy.

Nnamdi's father had been a good chief of police. Many times, the wives and mothers of people who his father had helped came to his house bearing gifts. Nnamdi would eavesdrop from the kitchen as these women thanked his father, while his mother brought iced tea or orange Fanta to drink. "Thank you, sir," one of the women sobbed. Thieves had once gutted her house when she was on vacation. Angry and disgusted, Nnamdi's father had personally investigated and pursued the case, and then he and a team of officers apprehended the thieves. "These stupid thieves are so cruel; you have the brave heart of a lion." The next day, the story was all over Kaleria's popular newsletter, the *Kaleria Sun*, and Nnamdi had gone to school so proud that day.

Nnamdi's father refused all bribes and his efforts were starting to result in a decrease in petty crime in Kaleria. He'd just turned his efforts toward the Chief of Chiefs, the apex of the town's crime. His father came home one evening, so excited. He'd talked about a big meeting he'd called at the department. He'd drawn charts on the dry-erase board as officers threw out ideas, and the department put together a great plan that would target each of the Chief of Chiefs' main cohorts while diplomatically approaching the Chief of Chiefs.

His father and the infamous Chief of Chiefs had sat down in the police station to discuss a compromise. Even the press was invited to witness this. The resulting news article was titled "The Meeting of Two Chiefs." During this meeting, the Chief of Chiefs promised to turn his energy toward combating the growing crime and corruption in Kaleria instead of fueling it. "You cannot build a palace in a ghetto," the Chief of Chiefs had been quoted saying. There was even a photo of the two men grinning and shaking hands. Two nights later, his father was murdered.

Father would want to spit at all these stupid people, Nnamdi thought. Everyone in the compound was staring at the Chief of Chiefs and his entourage. They breathed through their mouths and stood or sat frozen, as if they'd forgotten who they were. *Idiots!* Nnamdi thought. *Such a disgrace to stare like this.* He frowned when he realized he, too, was staring. He closed his mouth. Nearby, one of his uncle's wives was carrying her newborn and the child screeched. The sound made Nnamdi's heart jump; it reminded him of his mother's bloodcurdling scream when the police had told her his father had been killed. But first there was the bloody letter on the night of his father's murder. Nnamdi shuddered.

It was a Friday night, around eight o'clock, the time when his father usually came home. There was a loud knock on the door. *Odd*, Nnamdi thought. His father had his own keys, of course. When Nnamdi opened the door, he saw a letter on the ground. His name was printed on the envelope, so he picked it up and tore it open. He found a piece of paper, which he un-folded. His entire body went numb. The writing on the paper was brown red, not black or blue. Nnamdi blinked. He knew exactly what he was seeing, but it took several moments to fully register. The letter was written in blood and he wanted to drop it like a poisonous spider. Nothing written in blood could be good, especially when you were the son of the chief of police. He read:

> When you dine with the Devil, bring a
> long spoon. Tell your mother that your father's
> spoon was too short.
>
> Sincerely,
> The Chief of Chiefs

Nnamdi stood there, reading the letter over and over. As he read, his night grew darker, a shadow descending over him. He quickly looked up, breathing hard, sure someone was there. But he was alone. His father had told him before that the Chief of Chiefs was dangerous, powerful, and clever. When Nnamdi asked for more details about him, his father always looked very sad, shook his head, and said, "Someday, but not today." And now this super-dangerous man not only knew who Nnamdi was, but he'd written him a letter? He remembered looking out into the night, wondering if the Chief of Chiefs was hiding out there, too small to spot, deadly like the most venomous snake.

"What is that?" his mother had asked, coming up behind him and taking the letter.

As she read it, Mr. Oke, their lanky old gateman, came running from his post accompanied by Constable Ukoro. "I'm so sorry, Ma," Ukoro said, his beret clutched to his chest. "Your husband has been shot. He is dead." That was when Nnamdi's mother had screamed the terrible scream that still haunted his nightmares. According to lab test results, the letter had been written in goat's blood.

The next day, his father's death was front-page news in the *Kaleria Sun*. Nnamdi and his mother were appalled to see that the newsletter printed the Chief of Chiefs' words, even including a photo of the actual letter. To add insult to injury, Nnamdi was quoted in the article: " 'I'm terrified!' the eleven-year-old son of murdered Police Chief Egbuche Icheteka said."

Nnamdi was so mortified that he'd broken out into a cold sweat after reading it and had then hidden in his room that entire day. Police officers and investigators had come to their house the night of the shooting to ask questions. A man in jeans and a T-shirt had asked Nnamdi how he felt about the letter from the Chief of Chiefs. How was Nnamdi supposed to know the guy was a reporter?!

Now Nnamdi watched as the Chief of Chiefs chatted with the guests at his father's burial. His entourage of criminals was like a cackle of hyenas come to laugh at the corpse of a fallen lion. *I can't believe this*, Nnamdi thought, fire burning in his chest.

After a few minutes, the Chief of Chiefs approached Nnamdi and his mother. Nnamdi forced himself to move from behind to stand beside her. Every nerve in his body tensed and he felt sweat trickling down his face into his collar. He clenched his stomach muscles and hands to try to stop shaking, but it was no use.

The Chief of Chiefs was dressed in an immaculate flowing white agbada that made him look like a rolling snowball, and white trousers with golden cuffs. On his feet he wore white designer slippers that looked like they were made from clouds. If it weren't for his long, well-oiled black goatee and gold-rimmed glasses, he could have passed for an overdressed child. Nnamdi blinked. The man's short stature had blinded his perception for a moment. The Chief of Chiefs was no styl-ish child, he reminded himself. And that was when his eyes fell on the Chief of Chiefs' right hand. On his wrist he wore a white-gold watch, but on his right index finger . . . Nnamdi's heart jumped, unable to tear his eyes from the heavy gold ring.

Horror descended on him as he felt warm wetness in his pants. *Oh my God*, he thought. But he couldn't stop it from happening. He'd urinated on himself. He wanted to run into the house, but instead, he froze. Thankfully, he was wearing a long black caftan and black pants.

Nnamdi knew the ring was heavy because he'd held it before. It was solid gold and in the shape of a dragon eating its tail. An Ouroboros. He knew all this because it was his father's ring. His father had had that ring since starting as a police officer twenty-five years ago. Nnamdi had asked his father about it and had even tried it on a few times. It had his father's name engraved on the inside. Nnamdi frowned, his face hot and his wet pants itchy and cold. He glanced at where his father lay, but he couldn't bring himself to go and see if the ring was still on his finger.

"We've come to pay our utmost respects to Chief Egbu-che Icheteka," the Chief of Chiefs said to Nnamdi's mother. The man spoke with the clarity of a professor. "We're very sorry for your loss."

He held out a fat envelope to Nnamdi's mother. She

glanced at it with a pinched face and flared nostrils. Nnamdi held his breath. He only saw this look when his mother was about to lose her temper. Nnamdi's auntie Ugochi quickly reached forward and took the envelope. She opened it and glanced inside. Nnamdi leaned forward to see. The envelope was packed with money! Nnamdi shivered and became more aware of the wetness making his legs itchier. In a few minutes, he'd start to stink. *I have to get out of here*, he thought.

"Thank you," Auntie Ugochi quickly said, placing a hand firmly on Nnamdi's mother's shoulder. His mother softly hissed, biting her lip. "My sister is too distraught to speak."

"That is understandable," the Chief of Chiefs said. "Such a great man . . . shot down in the prime of his life. What will become of our Kaleria?"

Nnamdi's stomach churned with acid. The envelope was probably filled with thousands of naira or maybe even euros or American dollars. This man had killed his father and was now showering his mother with money. Nnamdi balled his fists, imagining punching the Chief of Chiefs in the face. His legs tensed as he considered kicking him in his privates. But instead, Nnamdi held himself still, squeezing his mother's hand.

He bit his lip hard as he watched the Chief of Chiefs amble off and mingle with some of Nnamdi's aunts and even members of the police department. His uncle Ike even hugged the Chief of Chiefs and begin talking animatedly with him, as if he were privileged to get the Chief's attention. How could any of them *speak* with him? At his father's funeral? How could his auntie not let his mother tell the man off? What was wrong with everyone? But Nnamdi himself also said nothing. *Look at me*, he thought, tears blurring his vision. *Daddy would be ashamed*. The moment his mother started talking to his aunt, he made for the house.

You won't get away with this, Chief, he thought to himself as he threw open the door. *None of you will! You will all be rotting in jail or dead by this time next year*. He had no idea what he was saying or what he'd do, but he'd do *something*. Just before going inside, he turned around and looked across the compound toward the tent where his father's body lay. Tears cooled his face. In the back of his mind, a snide voice said, *Stop talking big words. You think you're one of the superheroes in your comic books? Those are just simple idealistic stories and you're just a child.*

A hand fell on his shoulder and he jumped. The tension eased as he turned to see that it was his uncle Innocent. Nnamdi quickly wiped his wet face and tried to blink away his tears. "I know how you feel," Uncle Innocent said softly. "But take comfort; God will punish them."

That night, Nnamdi's mother was too upset to notice more than her own tears. But Nnamdi was alert. He'd noticed three things were missing. There had been one last can of tomato paste in the kitchen cupboard. Nnamdi remembered because his mother had mentioned that she wanted to go to the market for more as soon as everything settled down. It had been in the top right cupboard. It wasn't there anymore.

And in the bathroom the glass apple that sat on the toilet's tank was gone. His father had hated that apple and was always complaining about it. Whenever he saw it, his father humphed with irritation and said in his deep, gruff voice, "What is the point of an apple made of glass?!" As a way to playfully annoy his father, Nnamdi's mother had placed the glass apple on the tank of the toilet. Now it was gone.

And then there was the red pillow that his mother loved to put behind her back when she sat in the chair in the bedroom. It wasn't memorable in any way. It wasn't exceptionally lumpy, nor was it pretty or ugly. It wasn't given to her by anyone special. It wasn't very old or very new. It was just a pillow. And it was gone.

Who had taken these little things? Nnamdi was sure he knew. He was positive. The whole compound had been full of criminals. The thief was one of them. Maybe Mama Go-Slow or Never Die or Three Days' Journey. But certainly, it was upon the orders of the Chief of Chiefs. Stealing insignificant things from the house of the police chief he'd just murdered was icing on the cake.

Nevertheless, for now, Nnamdi knew he and his mother had to just make it to tomorrow. Without his father.

2

A Year Later

NNAMDI TOUCHED THE ant and it ran wildly behind one of the tiger lily's orange petals. Normally, Nnamdi avoided these large black ants. They had a painful bite. But today, he'd have almost welcomed the pain. Anything to get his mind off the fact that today was exactly a year since his father's murder. His *still unsolved* murder. He flicked the flower with his finger, knocking the ant and three of the wild lily's five petals to the ground. His father would have been angry with him for doing that. But his father was not here. The reality of this washed over him, warm and sour, yet again. He shut his eyes.

He went to the base of the mango tree and picked up his backpack. There were ants climbing all over it. This mango tree had always been occupied by them. His father used to say that if you tried to chop the tree down, the ants would probably attack you. Nnamdi smacked his backpack several times, then he closely inspected it to make sure the ants were all gone. He hoisted it onto his back. It was heavy with schoolbooks.

He sighed. The sight of his father's dying garden added to the weight in his heart. His father had planted this garden years before Nnamdi had been born.

"I had a dream," his father had told Nnamdi. "It was the night after I started as the chief of police. Oh, it was an awful dream. I saw Kaleria burning. The houses, the business buildings, the market, the cars on the roads. And as it was burning, it was being overrun by criminals like Never Die, Mama Go-Slow, and Three Days' Journey!" He chuckled. "I was under so much stress. Chief of police is a heavy job and I wanted to do it right. I had a friend in university who used to garden to relieve stress. If it worked for him, I thought, it could work for me."

And Nnamdi figured it must have, because his father never had the nightmare again. At least, not that Nnamdi knew of. Over time the garden became his father's place to relax. Nnamdi's mother said that after he became chief of police, the garden grew like crazy. The more Kaleria's well-being became his responsibility, the more he planted and cultivated and maintained. He even grew yams here. Nnamdi sometimes sat in the garden at the base of the palm tree that grew there and read comic books, but rarely did he garden with his father. It was an unspoken rule: These plants were his *father's* projects. You could hang out in his space, but only if you didn't mess with anything.

Since his death, not surprisingly, the garden had fallen into neglect. His mother did what she could, but she focused mainly on those plants that could feed her and Nnamdi: the tomatoes, peppers, and onions. She let the rest of the garden get overrun by weeds. As for Nnamdi, he rarely came out here at all. Now only wild grass, aggressively creeping touch-and-die plants, and tiger lilies were thriving here. He ran his toe over a bunch of touch-and-die plants and watched their fernlike leaves hastily close, the stems withering.

Nnamdi looked at his watch: school started in ten minutes. His mother would come looking out here soon. Still, he didn't move. His feet felt frozen, like when he'd seen the Chief of Chiefs.

"Nnamdi!" Chioma said, coming around the house. "Hurry up!"

She pushed her long untidy braids out of her face. Everything about Chioma Nwazota was long, from her gangly legs and arms to her bushy hair she usually braided herself. Nnamdi had known Chioma since they were babies. Where Nnamdi had always been on the quiet and intense side, Chioma was outspoken, upbeat, and playful. And she'd always been that friend who told him to move faster.

Chioma paused, staring at the garden. Nnamdi didn't think she'd been here since the funeral. Chioma was adopted and though her adoptive mother loved her to pieces, her father had never wanted to adopt her and told her so whenever he got the chance. Nnamdi's father, on the other hand, had always smiled when he saw Chioma and he happily gave her advice the many times she sought him out for it. Nnamdi's father had been more of a father to Chioma than any man. And Chioma was the only person Nnamdi had ever seen garden alongside his father. Knowing her, she'd probably just walked in on him one day and picked up a hoe (something Nnamdi never had the nerve to do), but that didn't change this fact.

"Nnamdi!" she called again. "What are you doing? We're going to be late."

"I'll walk fast," Nnamdi muttered.

"Let's start walking then." She hoisted up her backpack and turned toward the house.

School was the usual routine and Nnamdi was glad when the day was over. He just wanted to sit, think, and brood. But first he wanted to eat a little something. He was so hungry. During lunch, he'd been so preoccupied with the fact of his father being gone a whole year that he'd stared off into space instead of eating. *A whole year.* He hadn't spoken to his father in a whole year. He could say that now.

"You want one?" Chioma asked, offering him a biscuit from the package she'd just opened. "They're really *delicious.*"

Nnamdi took one. It was surprisingly buttery and flaky. He smiled. Chioma smiled, too, handing him three more. "That's better," she said. "No one wants to look at a long face."

They walked in silence for a moment and then Nnamdi asked, "You know what today is, right?"

"Yes," she said quickly. She handed him another biscuit.

He took it. "You're coming next week?" he asked.

"To Chief's memorial?" She always called his father "Chief."

Nnamdi nodded.

"Of course," she said, shoving a biscuit into her mouth. "Hey, remember that day in Chief's garden when I caught that huge blue butterfly?" Chioma asked. "He was watering the tomatoes and you were leaning against the fence?"

Nnamdi remembered that day well. It was three years ago. The garden attracted lots of butterflies and Chioma loved them. That late afternoon she'd caught and released a large blue butterfly and the sheer delight on her face as she watched it fly away made his father laugh. Great big belly laughs that soon got Nnamdi laughing, too, and Chioma rolling her eyes.

"Chief looked so tall that day," she said. "His shadow stretched and stretched like he was a giant. Like he was invincible." She glanced at Nnamdi and then looked away. "I really miss him." She handed him another biscuit and he ate it. A year since that terrible day. Almost a year since he'd made a useless, silly promise to himself while watching the Chief of Chiefs parade through his father's burial like the president of Nigeria.

"Well, how do you feel about . . . it?" she asked.

They were walking past the market. An old brown Toyota drove by, sending up a cloud of red dust that lingered in the hot, humid air. Nnamdi fanned the dust away, frowning. "I . . ."

"Whoo, Nnamdi," Chioma said, scrunching up her face. "Did you gas?"

Nnamdi hissed, annoyed. "No." Then he smelled it, too. Like rotten eggs. "Nasty," he said, flaring his nostrils.

"Phew! What is that?" Chioma asked.

"I don't know." But that wasn't quite true. *Could it be?* Nnamdi wondered. He frantically looked around for clues. Bad Market was known for causing a bad smell after he'd "collected" from people in the market. It was the cue to check your pockets and realize your valuables were long gone.

"Relax," Chioma said, eating another biscuit. "When Bad Market strikes, the smell comes fast and is *really, really* obvious. You won't just think farts; you'll think a monster farting in a nest of rotten meat! I have an auntie who was shopping once when he struck. She lost her wallet and wedding ring. And she said she never felt anything! But what she said was worst about it was the stink!"

Nnamdi only grunted. For the last week or so, he'd had a feeling that something bad was happening or had already happened somewhere. Today it was especially strong. Bad smells, faint or strong, always meant trouble. At least that's what his father used to say.

"Nnamdi," Chioma said. "You've been so quiet, even to me. What's on your mind, man?"

He paused, frowning. Then he looked at her concerned face, bit his lip, and spoke. "Okay, Chioma, honestly, I'm . . . I'm . . . I don't know. I just feel . . ." He looked hard at Chioma, wishing she'd just understand.

However, she only looked at him, waiting.

He sighed. "Remember when the Chief of Chiefs came to the burial?"

"Of course," she said, making a fist. "It was like he was rubbing it in your mother's face."

"And mine," Nnamdi added.

"We should find him and step on him," she said, dramatically stomping her foot on the ground. She grinned. "He's half of both our heights. We could take him."

Nnamdi chuckled sadly. "See, that's what I vowed to do that day. When he came, he made me so mad. I told myself I'd do something. But it's almost a year later and . . ." He shook his head. They stopped at the intersection and waited for several cars and trucks to pass. Then they ran across.

"So, is that why you're ashamed?" she asked as they

skirted around a burned-out car. Nnamdi wished someone would remove it. It was like a corpse. Actually, at one point, there *had* been a corpse inside it. Seven months ago, a drunk driver known all around Kaleria for nearly running people over had finally hit and killed a woman trying to cross the street. This was the last straw. Within a minute, an angry mob surrounded his car and set it on fire . . . with him inside. His father would *never* have allowed "jungle justice" to happen in Kaleria, let alone leave the burned-out vehicle on the side of the road. Times had certainly changed.

"I didn't say I was ashamed."

"I know," she said. "But I *know* you. You don't have to say it for me to know."

"What?" Nnamdi rolled his eyes and kissed his teeth. "I just think I should do something."

"About what? The Chief of Chiefs? The riffraff he works with? What *could* you do? Did you hear about Mama Go-Slow?"

Nnamdi nodded. "Yeah, she struck again yesterday, right?"

"At the height of evening traffic this time! The woman and her thugs are getting bold," Chioma said. "My neighbor Father Raphael lost an entire batch of holy water and holy bread! He said some masked person appeared out of nowhere inside his car and then the person, water, and bread were gone!" She pressed her left eye with her index finger. "In the blink of an eye!"

"Even holy things aren't safe," Nnamdi said.

"I know, right? My mother says this town used to be rich and now it's becoming rubbish. You have nothing to be ashamed of. Even your *father* couldn't stop these people and all the corruption."

They stopped at Chioma's apartment building. "Here, have the rest," she said, giving him the package of biscuits. Then she ran in. Nnamdi bit into one of the buttery biscuits as he watched her open the gate and go inside. She was right: Kaleria used to be rich. *But when the honey flows, the flies always smell it*, Nnamdi thought. His mother had said this the night after his father's murder, when she was in an especially dark mood.

"There must be something I can do," Nnamdi muttered as he headed home. "I'll bet if Daddy could, he'd fight them all as a ghost."

Nnamdi's home was surrounded by a concrete wall. It was topped with barbed wire and broken glass, and built into it was a red metal gate. Each time the gateman pushed the gate open, Nnamdi noticed its hinges were beginning to rust. It made his heart heavy because he knew that if his father were alive, they'd have had enough money to fix it.

"Mr. Oke," Nnamdi called. He hiked up his schoolbag and knocked on the gate. When there was no answer, he knocked again. He frowned. Mr. Oke, the gateman, was always at his post, ready to open or close the gate. He'd been their gateman for over twenty years. The old man was a dear friend of his father's. Even now that his mother could only pay him half of what he was paid before, he stayed on, living in the guest quarters.

"Mr. Oke, it's me! Nnamdi!" Still no answer. "Where *is* he?" Then he heard it, ever so faintly. Sobbing. It was coming from beyond the gate. From inside the house? Nnamdi's cheeks grew hot and a shiver leapt up his spine. He started banging like crazy on the gate. "Mr. Oke! Mr. Oke, are you there?! What is happening?! Mr. Oke!" A car slowly passed on the lumpy dirt road behind him. He didn't turn around to see who it was. He didn't care. "Mr. Oke!"

Finally, he heard footsteps approach the gate, the clang of it being unlocked, and there stood Mr. Oke, a worried look on his wrinkly brown face. "Come," he said, taking Nnamdi's hand.

"What's going on?"

"Your mother was robbed on her way from the market," he said. "In broad daylight!"

"What?"

They moved quickly across the compound. Mr. Oke opened the front door, and the sound of his mother's sobbing was loud and clear. She was sitting on the couch, her head in her hands. Nnamdi ran inside.

"Mommy!" He threw his arms around her and hugged her. She leaned on him and sobbed into his shoulder.

"Nnamdi, why did your father leave us, o?!" she wailed. "Why did he leave us to suffer, o?!"

Nnamdi felt tears prick his eyes. He'd never seen his mother in such a state, even on the day she learned of his father's death. No thief would have ever done this to her if his father were alive. Everyone knew who she was. But then again, his mother wouldn't have been reduced to selling tapioca if his father were alive. Nnamdi looked at Mr. Oke with questioning eyes, unsure of what to do. Mr. Oke just shrugged.

"Mommy, what happened?" Nnamdi asked. "Where is your tray of tapioca?"

She looked at him, wiping the tears from her cheeks, and then straightened up, pursing her lips. Nnamdi gazed at his mother's face. She'd become so dark now from all the time she spent in the sun, drying and then selling tapioca. A year after his father's death, the little money they had had dried up and the police had turned a blind eye to their slain chief's widow and son. Nnamdi had been unfamiliar with tapioca until his mother started selling it. He'd helped his mother arrange the shredded boiled stalks of cassava onto the tray every evening. "It's poor man's food," his mother had said. "People chew it to keep hunger away." They looked at each other and Nnamdi was sure she was thinking the same thing he was, that they were now in that group. Now something had happened to the food she sold to the poor.

"Mommy, what happened?"

"I dropped it," his mother said. "It . . . it was that hood-lum, the one they keep shooting who always lives. The one they call Never Die. He followed me and waited until I was alone on the road and then demanded all my money! He said if I didn't give it to him, he'd beat me right there on the road! I gave him all I had. Oh my God, what have I become, o?!" She started sobbing again.

"Get her some water," Mr. Oke said.

Nnamdi nodded and rushed to the kitchen, glad to get away for a moment. As he opened a bottle of cold water and poured it into a glass, he took a deep, angry breath. "Some man of the house I am," he grumbled. He closed his eyes. *If I could only buy her a car*, he thought. *Then at least she wouldn't have to walk in the hot sun the way she does and risk running into thieves.* Even as he'd spoken to her, he'd noticed her feet. They looked tough as leather, despite the protection of her sandals, and her bunions looked a lot worse. Anger heated his chest. Anger at the police who had abandoned them. Anger at his own powerlessness. And most of all, anger at the Chief of Chiefs.

He took the glass of water to his mother and watched her drink. "Thank you, Nnamdi."

He hugged his mother again.

Later, his feet took him to the back of the house, to his father's garden. He walked among the weeds and sat down.

His eye fell on a feeble but still living yam vine.

"I'll take care of you," he whispered to the plant. He'd take care of the whole garden from now on, he decided. He sighed and then he wished for one thing with all his heart: that he was a grown man who could protect his mother. As he caressed the yam's delicate green vine, he knew full well that it was a stupid wish.

3

The Ikenga

NNAMDI HATED THE brand-new scratchy white caftan and pants he had to wear and he resisted the urge to scratch in front of everyone. He was hot, the music was too loud, and he didn't want to talk to all these people. It seemed all of Kaleria had come out for the one-year memorial celebration of his father's life.

There were coolers full of jollof rice and goat meat, vegetable soup, spicy stew and pounded yam, fried plantain, and plenty of beer and palm wine. Free food, free festivities. Everyone was invited. And everyone came. It was nine p.m., and the party would probably continue well into the early morning. Nnamdi wondered how his mother could afford all this. He also knew that if he asked, his mother would only say, "God provides." Probably the women's club had paid for it. If that were true, he wondered why they didn't help out with money on other days.

His friends Ruff Diamond, Jide, and Hassan had come with their parents and siblings, of course. They stood near the wall, watching the guests mill about eating, talking, and dancing.

"Did you see that fine girl over there?" Ruff Diamond asked. He carried a plate of jollof rice and chicken in one hand and he shoveled some of the rice into his mouth with his plastic spoon.

"No," Nnamdi said, rolling his eyes.

"That's because you weren't looking hard enough," Ruff Diamond said. "Come on, have some fun. I'm tired of your sulking." He held a spoonful of jollof rice to Nnamdi's face. "Eat. It's delicious and you look dried like stockfish."

Nnamdi shoved the spoon away, cracking a smile. Debo Okunuga, known more commonly as Ruff Diamond, was bigger than Nnamdi, and each day after school he would bring out a pair of diamond earrings and put them on. "These teachers won't let me wear my diamonds in class," he would always say with a shrug. "Teachers, always jealous of rich guys like me!" Ruff Diamond was beyond proud of these earrings and claimed they cost two hundred and fifty thousand naira each. Nnamdi believed the earrings were expensive but not *that* expensive.

"Maybe you're too busy looking for Chioma?" Jide said, pushing up his black glasses as he drank from a bottle of Coca-Cola. Nnamdi rolled his eyes again. For over a year, Nnamdi had known that Jide was the one who liked Chioma, but Chioma never gave Jide the time of day.

"It's my father's memorial," Nnamdi said. "Why would I . . . ?"

"Because the best place to meet girls is at events like this," Hassan said. He put his plate, laden with only hunks of goat meat, on the ground just so that he could dramatically slap hands with Ruff Diamond. The two laughed raucously.

"Hey, I'm going to Abuja for a few days," Ruff Diamond said. "The girls are fine there, sha. But not like here. You should keep your eyes open, Nnamdi."

"So I can always remember that I met her at the anniversary of my father's murder?" Nnamdi suddenly snapped. He paused, feeling the darkness and weight of his father's death press on him yet again. His friends looked anywhere but at him. Nnamdi took a deep breath. "Sorry, guys," he said.

Ruff Diamond patted him on the back. "It's all right."

Nnamdi was glad when his mother called him over to come and say hello to his grand-auntie Grace.

"Praise God," Auntie Grace proclaimed, pulling him into a tight hug. She was very fat, tall, and strong and she wore a black drape of a dress made of a thick, coarse material. Hugging her was suffocating, hot, and scratchy. "Praise him, o! We are here today, gathered despite the loss of my sweet, sweet brother."

"Yes, Auntie," Nnamdi said, stepping back.

"Do you miss him?" she asked. Before Nnamdi could respond, she said, "I miss him. But he's with God now." She grinned at Nnamdi, though he knew full well that she wasn't really seeing him. Auntie Grace was nice, but she was never fully there; she was always more occupied with whatever prayer she was praying.

"I prayed for him every day when he was alive," she said. "When he was fighting all of those criminals. Trying to be Kaleria's superhero. Do you like superheroes, Nnamdi?" He opened his mouth to answer. He loved superheroes. Especially icons like Naruto, Superman, Black Panther, Storm, and his favorite, the Incredible Hulk. Superheroes got to view the world differently because their lives were so crazy; they could be *anyone* and they could dive into danger when it was at its worst and win. Superheroes survived. Nnamdi would have loved to have a conversation about all this with even Auntie Grace but instead she kept talking. "Your father wasn't a superhero; he was *more*. He was a messenger of God. Now he's with the Lord." She nodded, whispering, "He's better off."

Nnamdi frowned. He felt his father would have been better off with him and his mother. Auntie Grace's attention was back to his mother and two other women. "We should all pray!" Auntie Grace proclaimed, putting a big hand on his mother's shoulder.

Once his auntie started making people pray, those present lost at least an hour of their lives as she went on and on.

Nnamdi was standing behind her and he took the chance to slip away. He was between two tents, about to sneak away from the party, into the tall plants of his father's garden despite the mosquitoes and other night creatures, when he heard, "Nnamdi! There you are!"

He cringed but then recognized the voice over all the noise. "Chioma," he said, turning around. He smiled. Like most of the girls and women at the memorial, she was wearing a *rapa* and matching top; hers was a loud yellow. She moved slowly, her tightly wrapped rapa limiting the length of her stride. Nnamdi and Chioma slapped hands.

"I've been here for twenty minutes but couldn't find you anywhere," she said. She took a sip from her bottle of Bitter Lemon.

"I'm not in the mood for any of this," he said, leaning against the wall of the house.

"Hmm. Well, the party's more for your mother, really," she said. "To usher her out of mourning and back into the community. You should be relieved. She won't have to wear black anymore." She patted her belly. "Whoo, I'm stuffed."

"I'm glad for my mum, but I don't really want to be here."

"Oh, Nnamdi," she laughed. "You're such a good, obedient son."

A shadow caught Nnamdi's eye and he turned and squinted in the darkness. "You see that?" he asked.

Chioma craned her neck and squinted, too. "No."

"What is that?" He stepped past Chioma for a better look. "Or *who*?" The shadow was human-shaped and heading toward the gate, moving around the vehicles parked on the blacktop around the compound. "Hey!" he called. Whoever it was stepped into the light and seemed to look at them. But even in the light shining from the house, Nnamdi could barely see him. Yes, it was a him. A man. Then the man did the impossible. He stepped right through the wall beside the open gate! At least that's what Nnamdi thought he saw. The man skipped around the parked cars and disappeared from Nnamdi's view.

"Hey!" Nnamdi called again, pushing the gate open and stepping through it.

Behind him, he heard Chioma shout, "Leave him. You don't know who that is."

Nnamdi caught another glimpse of the shadowy man. He seemed to be walking quickly down the street, disappearing into shadows and reappearing in pockets of light from houses and streetlights. The man stopped and gestured to Nnamdi to follow. Nnamdi hesitated, frowning. He blinked, thinking of his dead father, his mother robbed, the Chief of Chiefs disrespecting his father's funeral last year, and something new washed over him. He tensed his body and balled his fists. "No," he whispered. "This is *my* house." He would protect his home by any means necessary. He took off after the shadowy man. "Hey!" he called.

"Nnamdi!" Chioma shouted. "It's dark out there! Stop! Just let him go!"

Nnamdi ran into the darkness of the dirt road, frantically looking from side to side. There. He heard the man's footsteps running off to the right, down the narrow track, and so he ran in that direction, too. The night was pitch-black as he passed gated house after gated house. The sound of the memorial celebration quickly faded, as did Chioma's voice. The wind picked up and it propelled him faster. It was exhilarating to run like crazy in the dark after . . . what? A thief? He didn't know. But now that he actually had a chance to do something, he was going to catch up with the man who had the nerve to come to his home uninvited.

He could hear his own breathing and the soft slap of his shoes in the dirt. His clothes were getting soiled, but he couldn't worry about that at the moment. He rounded a bend. Thankfully, he knew this road like the back of his hand, even in the dark. He wasn't far from where the old woman liked to fry and sell *akara*. He stopped and his legs shook with adrenaline.

There stood the man.

Yards away, under the streetlight.

Waiting?

Nnamdi's entire body was shaking. But as he stared at the shadowy man, he felt his heart leap. "Oh my God," he whispered. The man wasn't a shadow anymore. Nnamdi paused. Then he slowly walked toward him. The man was tall and wore black pants, a black long-sleeved shirt, and . . . a green beret. Nnamdi stopped, four feet away, his heart doing a dance in his chest. The man's back was turned. Standing about six feet tall, his shoulders were broad and slightly hunched forward. His hands were at his sides, the fingers thick and long. Nnamdi breathed through his mouth and shut his eyes. When he opened them, the man was still there. There was only one thing to ask. "Daddy? Daddy, is that you?"

The night was warm and dark. The streets were empty. Nnamdi's world had become the patch of land beneath the streetlight, the man, and himself. Nnamdi stepped into the light and the man turned around. Nnamdi's mouth fell open, the world swam around him, and then his vision cleared. He looked deep into his father's eyes.

"Nnamdimma, my son," his father whispered.

"But . . . you're dead," Nnamdi said. "I saw . . . your body at . . . at the funeral." The breeze blew, and right before his eyes he saw his father's chest and head grow transparent and then solid again. "Kai!" Nnamdi exclaimed. "You're a spirit, o!" He stepped back, thinking of how his auntie Grace often warned him about "the devil in disguise." The man's beret even had the silver elephant emblem in front. In his chest, Nnamdi felt the longing for his father like something pulling at his heart. He could even smell his father's cologne. *Run!* he thought. But he couldn't. He flexed his legs and then relaxed.

Tears came to his eyes. It had been a year, yet in this moment, the reality of his father's death washed over Nnamdi more strongly than he'd ever experienced. The moment left him breathless.

His father held up his hands and then dropped them back to his sides. He sighed. "I'm sorry I died, my son," he said.

Nnamdi's shoulders shuddered as he fought his emotions. Even with all the effort, he couldn't help starting to sniffle. His father's voice, his scent, his everything. He missed him so, so much. The words tumbled from him like overdue rain. "Mommy . . . they got Mommy," he blurted. "Last week. It was the guy they call Never Die! Mommy is . . ."

"I know."

"Mommy's had to start selling *tapioca*! And that's how . . ."

"I know," his father said more firmly.

"She curses you every day!" Tears dribbled from Nnamdi's eyes. "And . . . and I don't blame her! Why'd you have to go and get yourself . . . killed like that? Now Mommy has to struggle! No one respects her enough to protect her now. We're lucky we still have our house! The thieves will descend on us soon, Daddy! As revenge against you! You didn't finish what you started. And I can't do anything about it!"

Nnamdi took a step forward, his arms half-raised. Then he stepped back and just stood there, sobbing, his arms to his sides. No, he couldn't run into his father's arms. Not anymore.

His whole body prickled and clenched. Those days were over. His father did not move to comfort Nnamdi either. He, too, just stood there looking sad. After a few moments, Nnamdi asked, "Why are you here?"

"To give you something."

"Give me something?" Nnamdi wiped the tears from his eyes. "Give me what? What can you possibly give me now?"

"Do you wish to protect your mother?"

"Yes."

"And Kaleria, as a whole?"

Nnamdi frowned.

"No need to answer right now. It's too big a question. But you will have to answer it soon enough. I can at least give you what you need, regardless." He paused, looking hard at Nnamdi. "Hold your breath."

Nnamdi hesitated, his auntie Grace's warnings about devils, witches, and demons running through his mind yet again. He looked around. Still, not a car passed on the road. Not a person walked by. Even at night, this was bizarre. It was Saturday. The akara lady made most of her week's pay on this night. Where was she? Was this the devil bringing him to a secluded place where no one could save him from being tempted to evil? But deep in his gut, he felt this *truly was* his father, not the devil trying to deceive him. And hadn't his father always said to trust your gut? He took a deep, deep breath and held it.

"This object, this thing . . ." His father spoke softly as he knelt down and gathered what looked like a pile of dirt at his feet. "It will steal your breath if you breathe while I'm offering it. That is what I am told." He spoke in a monotone voice, as if he were doing a ritual. He gathered and gathered the dirt into a pile and then it began to gather itself. Nnamdi's eyes grew wide as he struggled not to breathe.

"An Ikenga," his father said, scooping up some of the dirt. In his ghostly hands, the dirt rippled like vibrating water. "Know your deep Igbo, my son. *Ikenga* means 'place of strength.' From me to you, my son. To you *only*. No one else is to touch this. It is *your* responsibility. It is yours alone." The dirt made a crackling sound as it fused itself into the shape of an ebony figure with two long spiral horns, seated on a stool grasping what looked like a machete in its bulbous right hand. In its left, which was much smaller, it carried what looked like a planet. Its face was fierce and focused ahead, as if it could see the future and it didn't like what it saw. Every surface of the object was etched with tiny symbols, except the piercing eyes and thick, unsmiling lips. His father picked up the Ikenga and blew softly on it.

"You can breathe now," his father said softly.

Nnamdi exhaled and then took a deep breath, filling his lungs. The smell of strong palm wine entered his nose and the sound of the blood rushing in his veins thumped in his ears. He looked at his father.

"This one is old, passed down over and over. It will guide your hand correctly if you calm yourself and focus on the tasks," his father said.

Nnamdi shook his head to clear it. "What tasks?"

"Hold out your hand."

Nnamdi slowly held out both of his hands.

"Not the left," his father snapped. "Only the right. You do not take the Ikenga with any other hand but the right, your *aka ikenga*."

Nnamdi frowned, an odd thought popping into his head: *"Any other hand"? Why not just say "right hand"? We only have two hands.* He brought down his left and slowly, his father set the Ikenga on the palm of his upturned right hand. It was warm, like something alive, and felt oddly heavy, as if it were full of water. It was larger than his hand and as solid as a ten-pound barbell. Nnamdi grunted and stumbled forward, working not to bring his left hand up to help. But even as he did this, the Ikenga was shrinking, growing lighter and lighter until it was smaller than the palm of his hand.

"There is no advice I can give you for this. I can only give it to you or not give it to you. I choose to give it to you. Chukwu only knows the rest, my son."

Nnamdi closed his hand around the warm object, more on instinct than anything else. He was looking up at his father, suddenly feeling light-headed and a bit queasy. When he spoke, it felt like he was speaking up from the bottom of a well with a mouth full of warm honey. His words came slowly: "But doesn't Auntie Grace say that . . ."

Everything went black.

Then he was there again.

His father was slowly fading away.

Nnamdi tried to speak, but his throat was burning as if he'd just swallowed hot pepper soup. He fell to his knees, but his knees were burning, too. And his right hand was burning, still grasping the Ikenga. His face, arms, belly. He shut his eyes. Every part of him felt like it was in flames. Panic. Regret. *Should have stayed within the gate*, he thought. This was some evil, had to be. Only evil could feel this painful. Maybe this man was the Chief of Chiefs in some sort of crazy disguise. Maybe, like his father, Nnamdi had been shot. Was this what his father had felt as his life drained away? A whimper escaped Nnamdi's throat as he curled into himself, trying to squeeze out the pain searing through his body.

The pain stopped. He looked at his right hand; the Ikenga was gone. Slowly, Nnamdi stood up. But the ground felt mushy . . . not there? He looked down and nearly screamed. He was floating. "What is . . . ?"

He inhaled and exhaled on the empty road. *At least I'm still alive*, he thought.

"Stop it!" a woman screamed. *Beeeeeeep!* The noise was coming from straight ahead. Up the road. In the dark. Nnamdi frowned. Yes, it was dark, but—but he could *see*. Like he was a cat.

"Stop it! Please!" the woman screamed. "Take whatever you want; just don't hurt me!"

Nnamdi felt a powerful combination of complete confusion and an instinct to help. The need was so strong that he was overcome with dizziness and nearly fell over. Instead, he stumbled against the wall beside him. He steadied himself, pressing a hand to the concrete. The wall was rough and grooved and . . . as he ran his hand over it, he could hear every grain of concrete and dirt on the wall rolling and crumbling beneath his palm.

"Get off me!" This time Nnamdi heard the woman so clearly that she could have been a few feet away. He heard her hand shoving against the person trying to hurt her. Then he heard a *slap!* And a male voice growl, "Get out!"

Still dizzy, Nnamdi took off toward the shouts, again following his instincts. He wildly ran along the side of the empty road, the shouts sounding as if they were just in front of him, yet nothing appeared. He turned a corner and there, finally, he saw the car. A shiny silver Mercedes with its headlights on. The engine was still running. There were barbed logs on the road and a car stopped before them. A man and a woman were struggling at the front door.

"Ged out b'fore I break your head!" the man yelled in a slurred voice.

He pulled at the young woman's arm, but she held fast to the inside of the door. *What is . . . ?* But there was no time to process any of it. The woman was in trouble. Thinking of his mother at the mercy of a criminal like this, Nnamdi ran at the man and grabbed the collar of his shirt. *What am I doing?* Nnamdi thought with terror. *This man is going to tear me apart!* But Nnamdi yanked at the shirt anyway. *Maybe the woman will at least get away,* he thought. Even in the darkness, Nnamdi could see the drunken man's shirt was filthy, stiff with dirt, grime, and sweat. And he could smell him. Like putrid garbage and unwashed socks.

Nnamdi looked deep into his eyes: they were dreamy and unclear, like milk mixed with too much water. Nnamdi knew who this man was, as he knew all the crazies of Kaleria. This was Three Days' Journey, the dirty carjacker, who, despite his constant drunkenness, managed to steal close to a hundred cars each year. He would take the cars to Tse-Kucha, a town three days' journey away, where he would sell them for a nice price. Now, somehow, Three Days' Journey seemed to be having trouble pulling away from Nnamdi's grasp.

"Leave her alone!" Nnamdi shouted, yanking Three Days' Journey back and throwing him to the dirt. Nnamdi vaguely noticed the deep, echoing sound of his voice, but he was too focused on Three Days' Journey to wonder about it. As Nnamdi moved toward the wild man, several things dawned on him at once.

1: Three Days' Journey, a grown man of over six feet, was scrambling away from him, a twelve-year-old boy.

2: The low voice had been his own.

3: The woman behind him had shut the car door, turned the car around, and driven off.

"Please! AYEEEE! Don't hurt me, o!" Three Days' Journey shouted as Nnamdi stood over him. "Whooo!" Three Days' Journey jumped up, wobbling about. "I was just . . . please! Devil! Spirit! Whatev'r you are! Spare me, o!"

Nnamdi couldn't believe how wildly this man was behaving. He was screeching and dancing about like a madman. *Because of me?* he wondered. "Calm down! I'm just . . ."

"*Chineke!* You don' have to speak! Ah, ah! I've learned my lesson!"

Nnamdi frowned and took a small step toward Three Days' Journey, holding out a hand. "Let me help you," he said.

"AYEEEEE!" Three Days' Journey screeched. Then he turned and fled into the patch of nearby bushes, his long, skinny arms in the air like a terrified orangutan.

Nnamdi stood there in the darkness. He could clearly see Three Days' Journey shambling off through the bushes as if he were looking at him in broad daylight. The man tripped and fell, got up, and continued running away. *How can I see that?* Nnamdi wondered. Then he remembered how strongly he'd held the man. He looked down at his hands and gasped. They were the hands of a grown man! A large man, dark-skinned. Not "dark"—*black*-skinned, as if he were stitched from the night. He touched his face and felt stubble. He gasped, pulling his hand away with horror. "My body, o! My body, o!" he cried. He twitched, hearing his low, deep voice. "What's happened to me?! Witchcraft?"

Nnamdi turned and ran home.

He ran past people strolling on the roadside. Market women returning from a late night. More people headed to his compound for the party. He looked around, breathing frantically, wondering what he must look like. Where had they been when all this was happening? Cars and trucks passed him on the street. All he heard was his own breathing, like some huge man, and the sound of his huge feet slapping the dirt. He wasn't floating high above the ground; he was just super-tall. He briefly wondered what clothes he was wearing, for surely his own clothes were too small. He didn't look down to check.

His breathing grew faster and faster, and soon he was hyperventilating. His vision rolled around him, stars of red, silver, and blue bursting before his eyes as he finally arrived at his gate. He stumbled between the parked cars. He moaned, his vision blurring. Then, right there at the gate, he passed out.

❤ ❤ ❤ ❤

"Nnamdi!"

Someone was shoving him.

"Nnamdi! Wake up!"

He felt someone grab his shoulder and shake. He didn't want to open his eyes, afraid of what he would see. His chest ached, his throat burned, and a stone was grinding into the small of his back.

"What happened to you?" Chioma asked, her voice heavy with concern. She shook him again. "I know you're awake. Get up before someone *sees* you!" She grunted as she tried to pull him up. "Do you want to scare your mother?"

That reached him. Nnamdi slowly opened his eyes to see Chioma leaning over him. He sat up. "Ooh," he grunted, the blood rushing from his head. "Do I . . ." He paused. His voice sounded normal. "Do I look okay?"

Chioma grinned, looking him over as he slowly got up. "No blood," she said. "You have ten fingers and probably ten toes. You're fine!"

Nnamdi chuckled despite himself. "Yeah, I'm fine."

He was lucky to not have been run over by one of the cars. *Maybe I wasn't out for that long*, he thought. It was dark here, but his clothes were white; well, now they were a dirty white. And, he noticed, not torn. *Maybe it was all a dream.* He felt a sinking disappointment in his gut.

"What happened?" she asked. "Did that strange man

beat you for following him?" She frowned. "But you don't seem hurt."

"You saw him?" he asked louder than he'd wanted to.

"Yeah."

"Clearly?"

"Barely, but yeah. It was a man, I know that. I tried following you when you were running, but it was so dark and you just took off!"

He blinked and frowned. "Yeah, I don't know why I did that."

She nodded. "It was kind of stupid."

"Maybe."

They looked at each other until Nnamdi looked away. What was he supposed to tell her? He looked at the spot where he'd fallen and froze. Slowly, he knelt down and picked it up. "Oh my God," he whispered. The Ikenga. Immediately the aroma of strong palm wine descended on him. It had all really happened.

"What's that?" Chioma asked, taking it from him before he could stop her.

"Hey! Don't touch it!"

"Why?" She laughed, holding it up in her right hand. "Is this . . ." She brought it closer to her eyes. The smile dropped from her face as the Ikenga's head seemed to twitch. She screeched, shuddered, and shoved it back into Nnamdi's hands. "What is that? Something from your father's bookshelf? Oh wait, maybe it's a Nigerian action figure. Do they make those yet? Let me guess his name: Cosmic Juju Man!" She laughed.

He quickly put it in his pocket. "It's nothing."

Chioma looked from her hand to Nnamdi, shaking her hand as if the Ikenga had left some residue on it. "Seriously, though, what is it?" she said. "I don't like it at all."

Nnamdi shook his head, babbling, "No, no, it's not . . . it's just . . ."

"Nnamdi, Chioma. Why are you two out here?"

They both turned around.

"Uncle Innocent," Nnamdi said, his voice too high.

"Good evening," Chioma blurted, wiping her hand on her dress.

"Nnamdi, where is your mother?" his uncle asked in his gruff voice. Nnamdi had always thought he sounded like a lion. He'd always hoped he would grow up to have the same voice. A voice that made people stop and listen.

"She's inside the house," Chioma said, pointing behind them.

Uncle Inno frowned at Nnamdi. "What happened to your clothes?"

"Oh . . . I . . . uh, fell."

Looking unsure, his uncle Inno said, "Go clean up."

"I will, Uncle," Nnamdi said.

As soon as Uncle Inno went inside, Chioma and Nnamdi went and sat on the bench away from the party.

"What happened to you?" Chioma asked.

"I don't . . . know."

"How can you not know? It was only a few minutes ago," she pressed.

He sighed. "Chioma, please. I . . . I need to think."

"Who was that man?"

"I . . ." He shook his head again.

She narrowed her eyes at him, then she sighed. "It's okay. Tell me later."

He nodded.

"You're okay, though, right?"

"Yeah."

"I'm going to go dance then. Your uncle was right—you should go change."

4

Wonder

IT WAS JUST past midnight and Nnamdi was finally alone. On his bed. In his room. He was Nnamdi again. But that didn't make sense; who else would he be? And who was he *really* now? *What* was he?

Nnamdi rubbed his temples as he sat on his bed. Had he really seen his father and then beaten up one of the most notorious carjackers in Kaleria? Three Days' Journey had looked at him and *cowered*. He'd pleaded for his life! Then Nnamdi had flung the big man aside like a piece of paper. And Nnamdi had felt . . . he'd felt strong, like some sort of superhero! Like his favorite hero, the Hulk!

He was twelve. Right now. How old would he be when the *spell* came upon him again? *If* the spell came upon him again.

He got out of his bed and walked to his bedroom window, where he looked out into the darkness. The darkness that no longer seemed as scary anymore. Not when he could become what he was earlier this night. Thieves would cower before him. Murderers would bow at his feet and beg to be locked up. *If* it happened again. And what was it? He didn't like not knowing.

He picked up the X-Men pencil case sitting on his night-stand, on top of his most valuable possessions: his one and only Naruto graphic novel and stack of Incredible Hulk comic books. Slowly, he brought the Ikenga from his pocket. It was still warm, and holding it sent a sort of electrical current through his hand that made his fingers slightly curl and the muscles ache. And it still smelled of palm wine, something his father had loved to sip after particularly stressful days. Nnamdi put it into the case and placed it on top of his stack of Hulk and Naruto books. As he drifted into sleep, he felt uneasy.

His dreams were full of smoke and heat and screams. *Kaleria was on fire. The houses and buildings. There was the crash of glass as groups of thugs laughed and entered a burning building and then came out again. One single man carried an entire refrigerator. Another carried a screaming woman. Still another carried three large flat-screen televisions stacked one on top of the other. Nnamdi stood there, watching it all happen. But he was nothing but a shadow behind the flames.*

He awoke hearing the happy Sunday morning chatter of his mother, his auntie Ugochi, and uncles Egbe and Inno from downstairs. He lay there. The air in his room was clear, smoke-free. No one was screaming. Everything was fine. He was holding his breath. He opened his mouth wide as he let it out.

"Just a dream," he muttered. "Thank goodness."

Nnamdi came down the stairs to find his mother and auntie in the kitchen, huddled around the *Kaleria Sun* newsletter on the table. Nnamdi greeted them and sat down, wondering what was for breakfast. He was starved and he smelled fried eggs. He peeked at the newsletter headline and immediately lost his appetite.

The headline read: "Three Days' Journey Thwarted in Three Seconds."

There, on the front page, was a picture of a grinning woman, the very woman he'd saved last night.

Tina Adepoju, a mother of three who drives a silver Mercedes, had stopped when she came across a spiked log lying in the road. Before she knew it, the infamous carjacker Three Days' Journey set upon her car. He threw her door open and tried to drag her out, but not before she could lay on her car's horn. As she struggled with Three Days' Journey, something happened. "This enormous . . . man! He just came out of nowhere," Adepoju said. "He was tall like an iroko tree, very dark-skinned, and very strong. He threw

Three Days' Journey to the ground like the rubbish he was!" Whoever this man is, I hope he's from Kaleria. And if he's not, let him come and live here.

Three Days' Journey was given his name because it's believed that he drives the cars he steals to a secret chop shop "three days' journey" from Kaleria. He first . . .

Nnamdi sat back with wide eyes. He felt an odd tingle in his throat. The news story was not very accurate about what he'd looked like and he didn't remember hearing a horn, but it told him one clear truth: He'd done something terrible yet wonderful. Him. He had caused this woman to gush with happiness to reporters. He had saved someone from being yet another victim of Kaleria's crime problem. His mother, aunt, and uncles were smiling. His father would be proud.

"The story sounds as if Nnamdi's father was out there last night!" Auntie Ugochi said.

Nnamdi's mother nodded. "Especially the part about throwing Three Days' Journey. Egbuche really disliked that man," his mother said with a chuckle.

"Mommy," Nnamdi said, getting up. He needed some air to clear his mind and think. "I'll be right back."

"Don't be too long," she said. "Your food will get cold."

My father, Nnamdi thought as he quickly watered the garden. *Did he really come back?* He felt like going to his room

right now and touching the Ikenga once more and imagining he was touching his father's hand through it. He paused,
looking at the garden. He'd pulled most of the weeds, turned
the soil around the yam, and planted some sunflower seeds
Chioma had given him years ago. He'd purposely not told her,
because he wasn't sure if they'd grow. Plus, he wanted them
to be a surprise, if they did. He'd been tending to the garden
for days, and already the garden looked in better shape than
it had all year. His eye fell on the yam and he grinned. Several
new leaves had unfurled from the snaking vine.

He would tell no one about what had happened last night.
Not yet. Not even Chioma. Only his father knew his secret,
and it was nice to share a secret with his father.

5

Beneath the Palm Tree

IT SEEMED AS if everyone were reading a copy of the day's paper. People standing on the side of the road waiting for the bus, market women, people on their porches. When Nnamdi got to school, it was more of the same. Teachers stood in small groups, newsletters in hand, giggling and smiling and quoting sections of the story.

"The man is such an idiot," one of the teachers said. "Serves him right. I hope that man knocked Three Days' Journey's teeth out when he threw him aside."

And the story wasn't just in the *Kaleria Sun*, either: Ruff Diamond said it was also in newspapers from neighboring towns. "My uncle brought a newspaper from Aba and it was even in there!" The story had traveled far! Nnamdi put his chin to his chest and rushed off to the palm tree that grew in the middle of the school grounds. As usual, Chioma was there. She was sitting, reading a newsletter with a big grin on her face. She laughed loudly and pushed back her untidy braids. "This is crazy," she whispered.

"*Kee ka Ḍmee?*" Nnamdi greeted her in Igbo, leaning against the tree.

"You read this?" she asked, pointing to her paper.

"Who hasn't?"

"It's hilarious! Three Days' Journey getting tossed like a sack of dry grass?" She giggled again. "This is the best news Kaleria has had in a long time!"

"Heh, yeah," Nnamdi said. His lips felt chapped as he smiled.

Chioma squinted at him and folded her newsletter. "So are you going to tell me what happened last night? Come on, Nnamdi. I know you. You're hiding something."

"No," he said, looking out at the other students, who played and chatted nearby.

"No, what?" she asked. "No, you're not going to tell me what happened or no, you're not hiding something?"

Nnamdi sighed heavily. Chioma shielded her eyes against the sun and looked up at him. "Talk. You tell me everything. I'm not enjoying this new secretive side of you."

Nnamdi frowned.

"You didn't tell your mother you passed out, did you?" she said.

"No," he said, sighing loudly. "She has enough to worry about. Look, Chioma, I'm fine. Stop asking."

After a pause, she said, "Okay, o. So about the incident last night . . . it had to have happened close to where you were. You were lucky you didn't run into Three Days' Journey."

"Yeah."

"I told you not to leave the gate."

"I know."

She paused, again. Nnamdi bristled, sure that she was going to start badgering him about what had happened last night or about the Ikenga.

"Why do your fingers look like that?" Chioma asked.

"Like what?" he asked, looking at his hands.

"Dirty."

"Oh." He laughed, picking at them. "I've been . . . I've been working in my father's garden."

They both paused.

"Have the butterflies returned?" she asked quietly.

Nnamdi shook his head. In all his time weeding, watering, planting, and pruning back there, he hadn't seen one butterfly. He hadn't really thought much of this until Chioma pointed it out. Now it made his heart ache.

Chioma got up. "Let's go find Ruff Diamond. I want to hear his take on the Three Days' Journey incident." She giggled.

"Mmmm, okay." Nnamdi liked Ruff Diamond well enough, but he didn't quite trust him because of how much Ruff Diamond loved to exaggerate and embellish everything.

He'd be stung by a fly, but when he told you about it, the fly would turn into some enormous, rare blue bumblebee. Or he'd always just happened to be a block away from big things that happened. Nnamdi didn't care for his wide mouth, but Chioma always enjoyed his nonsense regardless of how little of it was true. They found Ruff Diamond chatting with a group of boys outside a clothing shop. Ruff Diamond waved and came right over when he saw them.

"You caught me just before I have to leave again," Ruff Diamond said.

"What do you mean? Your mother is back already?" Chioma asked. "But you were just at her house!"

"Yep. I hear my parents had a big fight, again. One day I'm there, then the next I'm here," he said with a lopsided smile. "That's divorce, I guess. Two big homes, two schools."

"Oh, poor you," Chioma said, rolling her eyes.

"Nah, I'm rich, not poor," Ruff Diamond said, smirking.

Nnamdi bristled so hard that his armpits prickled. Ruff Diamond was *so* annoying. "Well, you didn't miss much," he muttered.

"Ha ha, you're funny, man," Ruff Diamond said. "But you're right. I almost stepped directly into the trouble. We got home last night probably at the same time Three Days' Journey was attacking," he said as they walked into school. "We were probably a few houses away, about to reach home. My mom was driving the black Jaguar. I'll bet Three Days'

Journey would have attacked us if he saw our car first."

"It happened near *my* house," Nnamdi said. "You live fif-
teen minutes away."

"All I'm saying is that we were lucky last night," Ruff
Diamond insisted, annoyed.

"Nnamdi's the one who's lucky," Chioma said. "He was
out there, probably less than a block from where it happened,
as it was happening!"

"Did *you* see anything?" Ruff Diamond asked, cocking
his head.

"*I* think he did," Chioma said.

"Chioma," Nnamdi groaned.

"Well, what'd you see?" Ruff Diamond pressed.

"Nothing," Nnamdi said. Chioma opened her mouth to
say something, but when Nnamdi met her eyes, she instantly
shut her mouth, frowning. *Good*, he thought. *Glad she can
be quiet sometimes.* He felt a pinch of guilt; he didn't like the
look on her face. She almost looked scared.

"Well, if you did, I'll bet you could make a lot of money
telling the press," Ruff Diamond said. "They'd pay even a kid
for information, I think."

Chioma was still looking at him.

"I didn't see anything," Nnamdi insisted. "It was dark. A
lot of people were out last night."

6

Bad Market

AFTER SCHOOL, NNAMDI and Chioma walked home along the busy street. Cars zoomed by. Banana and bread hawkers screamed their wares, their large trays balanced on their heads. Auto mechanics cooled off beneath mango trees, drinking cold water from small plastic bags. It was a breezy afternoon and Nnamdi felt so good that for a moment he forgot about the night before. Then he made eye contact with a tired-looking woman selling bread and he thought of his mother selling tapioca. He felt terrible and . . . guilty. His mother would be returning from the market about now, alone and unprotected, and here he was having a fun walk home with a friend.

And if the newspapers would pay him for information about last night, what would be so crazy about going and telling them something? He could give every naira to his mother. That would be less time she spent selling tapioca at the market.

He could always say that he saw a shadowy man attack Three Days' Journey and save the woman. Technically, he wouldn't be lying. He'd seen his dark hands. But then, when the paper was published, he'd get more questions from Chioma and his mother. He'd get more questions from everyone. And then, at some point, he knew he'd have to start lying. It wasn't worth the risk.

"Let's go see if we can find my mother," Nnamdi said.

"At the market?" Chioma asked.

"I want to make sure she's . . . okay," he said.

Chioma nodded and he was glad. He didn't want to do any more explaining.

When they got to the market, they didn't have to look hard. There she was, walking past the booths and tables with her tray of tapioca on her head. Nnamdi felt another pinch of guilt. No one would have believed his mother could sink so low. She used to be the wife of the chief of police. People like her didn't have to work. People like her kept many of the market women in business by buying what they sold.

Nnamdi watched from a distance as his mother walked. People stopped and stared. Even a year later, people here still hadn't gotten used to seeing her as one of them. She must have felt it. Nnamdi certainly did. Shame. Again he thought about the money he could get from the newspapers . . . and he thought of the Chief of Chiefs, who'd caused all this.

"Mommy," he called, waving his hand. He and Chioma ran to her.

She smiled wanly. The armpits of her yellow blouse were damp with sweat and her feet were caked with dust. She walked slowly, wincing with each step. Nnamdi cringed. His mother had terrible bunions on both feet.

"Good afternoon, Mrs. Icheteka," Chioma said.

"Good afternoon, Nnamdi, Chioma," she said as Nnamdi quickly took her tray. "Thank you, Nnamdi." She stretched her back and Nnamdi could hear her joints pop.

"Mommy, you can't do this anymore. You look—"

"How was school?" his mother asked, cutting him off.

"Okay," he mumbled. She put her arms around both of their shoulders and they started walking home together.

They'd walked past several market stalls when Nnamdi smelled something utterly rotten. It was so rancid that he swooned with dizziness and nearly dropped the tray. The air itself took on a noxious green tint, like stinky fog. The stench was thickest in the market, tumbling out from between the stalls.

"Phew! What is that?" Chioma exclaimed, pinching her nose. "Oh my God! Nasty!"

His mother grabbed Nnamdi's arm and, when he looked at her, he knew they were thinking the same thing. She was the chief's wife and he was the chief's son. They both knew exactly what was happening and who had caused it. Then Nnamdi remembered the Ikenga . . . and what it could do.

"Chioma," Nnamdi said. He wriggled his hand from his mother's grasp. "Take this." He shoved the tapioca tray into her arms. "Stay with my mother! Please."

"No problem," she said, her voice sounding nasal because she was pinching her nose. "You're not going in there, are you?!"

"Nnamdi!" his mother snapped, trying to grab his arm again. "Where are you going?"

"I . . . I just want to go see," he said, stepping away. He'd never been a very good liar.

"Where . . . what are you going to do?" Chioma asked.

"Just stay with my mother!" he said.

"Nnamdi!" his mother screeched in a voice that made Nnamdi cringe. "Where are you going?"

Nnamdi ran into the green fog.

He coughed and leaned forward, putting his hands on his knees. Everything was stinky green haze. He could barely see three feet in front of him. However, he could hear people stumbling about and coughing.

"Bad Market," he whispered. That was who was behind this. Nnamdi remembered his father's description perfectly: "Bad Market is the head of a small but very crafty group of pickpockets," Nnamdi's father had explained to him only months before his murder. "When Bad Market finishes a job, he gets arrogant. He likes people to *know* they've been robbed; that's part of the thrill for him. He has these balloons filled with chemicals. He throws them when he is done robbing, and when they hit the air, that creates the smelly fog he is known for."

Nnamdi's father had said that Bad Market was a tall man who looked like a fashion model. He was light on his feet and therefore able to outrun authorities in all the confusion.

"Light on his feet," Nnamdi whispered. "Think. Gotta think." Nnamdi took a deep breath and relaxed his shoulders. *What's my task? What's my task? What's my task?* he thought. *What do I need to do?* He whispered, closing his eyes, "Find Bad Market." There was a brief pause in which he heard a fly buzz past his ear and a car honk its horn from nearby, then he felt himself . . . shift.

A coolness settled on his shoulders. His body felt as if it moved to the left, just a tiny bit. Then his senses opened up. He felt his nostrils expand and the terrible smell grew so full that it was like an actual taste on his tongue. And he felt his ears expand and suddenly he could *hear* everything. People bickering about whether to run or hide, babbling in fear, or shouting angrily as they discovered that their jewelry, shopping, and money were gone. He honed in on the sound of feet. Little feet. Children running. He strained harder. There. Bigger feet.

"That's Bad Market," he said out loud. He gasped. His

voice was so low. He opened his eyes. At first, all he saw was green. Then, as his powerful eyes adjusted, he began to see more. A woman was on her knees, feeling around for whatever she'd lost. A child to his right was standing there, crying. Nnamdi wanted to help, but he knew the best way to help was to focus. As he worked to do so, he looked down at his body. "Oh God," he whispered. He was a piece of outer space in the shape of a man. "What is . . . Wow." He pressed at his arm; it felt like an arm but looked like blackness blending into blackness.

Focus, he thought again. He shut his eyes. *To kill the snake, you cut off its head.* It was what his mother was fond of saying when she talked about how she felt one should fight Kaleria's crime. Nnamdi had never understood it and he still didn't. But the idea was fierce and it gave him strength. Focus. Slowly, the noise of chaos fell away and his ears pinpointed the sound of swift, nimble adult feet. Without opening his eyes, he took off in pursuit.

He was like a bat using sonar, seeing with sound. Eyes closed as he ran, all he had to do was listen. He ran past people and around corners and market stall dividers. He leapt over a dog. He didn't lose the sound of the swift footsteps. They were running faster now but also growing louder. Bad Market was fast, but Nnamdi was faster. He was closing in. Closer. Closer . . .

Nnamdi opened his eyes just in time to see the back of

Bad Market's suit jacket and sacks full of stolen items over his shoulders. Through the stench of the green fog, Nnamdi could smell Bad Market's designer cologne. He moved closer, reached out, and then grabbed him. They both went tumbling. The sacks of stolen naira, watches, rings, and necklaces went flying and fell onto a pile of firewood.

Bad Market tried to roll from beneath him, but Nnamdi was too big. Nnamdi snatched up Bad Market's arms and held them together as the limber man tried to squirm from his grasp. Nnamdi was so strong that he was able to drag the kicking and twisting Bad Market and lift him off the ground.

He held Bad Market up to his face. Nnamdi remembered his father describing Bad Market as tall, about six two. However, Nnamdi was a giant, standing probably a foot taller. Bad Market flailed about for a moment, then he looked into Nnamdi's face and screamed wildly. Then he . . . fainted. After all the thrashing and shrieking, the sudden silence was almost ridiculous to Nnamdi. He frowned and inspected Bad Market, then he dropped him with disgust. *What kind of grown man faints?* Nnamdi wondered. But then again, what kind of "man" did *he* look like?

The smelly green fog was dissipating and, though they were in a secluded section of the open-air market, Nnamdi sensed people nearby. What could he do? Tie up Bad Market, he decided, and get out of there before anyone saw him. He was looking around for something to use when Bad Market suddenly leapt up, grabbed a log of firewood, and smashed it against the side of Nnamdi's head. "YAH!" Bad Market shouted triumphantly.

Nnamdi stumbled backward, blinking and shaking his head. Bad Market was taller than his father, but very lean. He was dressed like the men Nnamdi saw on billboards and his face was twisted as he raised the log to beat Nnamdi some more. On instinct, Nnamdi caught the other end of the log with one hand and slapped Bad Market hard across the face with his other. Bad Market flew back as fast and powerfully as a kicked football. When he landed, he didn't move. "Oh no," Nnamdi whispered. He crept up to Bad Market's limp body and nudged him with his shadowy foot. Bad Market still didn't move. He nudged harder. Nothing. Quickly, the fog was disappearing and he saw four or five people standing there, staring.

"This is Bad Market," Nnamdi announced. He fought back the embarrassed giddiness he felt at his rich, deep voice. *They don't know*, he assured himself. *They just see a big shadow man.* He straightened up so that he stood much taller than he felt, and looked at an old woman, who whimpered and stepped back. Three men stood there but made no move to help. *Oh God*, Nnamdi thought. *I hope he's not dead.* He paused. Then he finally knelt down and shoved Bad Market onto his back. Bad Market rolled over, his eyes closed and mouth hanging open as it let out a loud snore. Nnamdi sighed with relief. He was just sleeping. Someone tapped Nnamdi on the arm. When he looked to the side, he saw the old woman.

"Here, take this," she said, handing him a scarf, scowling at him with narrowed eyes. She crept back, her eyes still on him. There had to be ten people around him now. All seeing him. He suddenly felt cold. Then he felt as if all his muscles were relaxing. He was changing back. Quickly, he tied Bad Market's limp hands with the scarf. Then he ran off.

Nnamdi breathed heavily as he fled. He felt the shadow self slipping from him and the feeling left him light-headed, as if he'd been hanging upside down. He rushed behind a house and sat down hard with his back against the wall. He could feel it; he was not himself yet. He could feel the length of his legs and arms. He could see his flesh, black like outer space in a *Star Wars* movie. However, his muscles felt mushy and weak. He wheezed and coughed. Suddenly, a force lifted him off the ground and slammed him to the floor. "Ooof!" he grunted, the little air in his lungs knocked out. As he lay there in the dirt, he wondered what would happen next. Was this his father? Was the power that had been controlling him going wrong? He'd hurt Three Days' Journey, too. Was God punishing him for harming yet another person? He pressed the heels of his palms to his eyes, trying to shake away the image of Bad Market flying back fast and hard because of Nnamdi's slap. Nnamdi had never slapped anyone in his life. God would punish him for sure.

When nothing more happened, he coughed again and

slowly pulled himself upright. He leaned his head against the wall and looked down at his school clothes. Filthy. At least the shadow hadn't eaten them away. Still, his mother was going to be so angry. He gasped. He had to get back to his mother and Chioma. They were probably still outside the market, worrying about where he'd gone.

He was about to get up when he heard soft chuckling. He froze, his mouth hanging open. It sounded like it was right beside him. But there was nothing there. "It's okay, son. Be more careful," he heard his father say. Nnamdi tensed up, his eyes wide. Then he heard his father's laughter, low and musical. Nnamdi listened as it faded into the distance. As if . . . as if his father were walking away.

"I won't hurt anyone again," Nnamdi said to the space around him. Only a brown goat tethered to a pole nearby responded. "Baaaah."

A peacefulness spread over Nnamdi and he changed completely back to himself and collapsed onto the dirt, overcome with a pounding headache and deep fatigue. This time he didn't pass out. With lidded eyes, he stared at his now small shaky dark-brown-skinned hands.

"No," he said to himself. "I won't hurt another person."

"Oh, thank God!" Chioma exclaimed when Nnamdi found them.

Once the smelly green fog had cleared, Nnamdi's mother and Chioma had walked all over the market, looking for him.

They told him how they saw people who'd fallen or bumped into each other or tumbled over things in the heavy fog. They'd seen people standing in line as police gave them back their things. And, like everyone in the area, they'd witnessed the capture of Bad Market.

"You missed all the excitement!" Chioma said. "Well, so did we, but we got to see the police shove Bad Market into a police car. He's really good-looking."

Nnamdi rolled his eyes. Chioma was always pointing out "good-looking" men.

"I wish they would catch Never Die," his mother growled, and Nnamdi knew she was remembering how he'd robbed her on her way home from the market. "So, what happened to you in there?"

"I guess I kind of just got lost in the fog," he said with a laugh that sounded false even to him. He avoided Chioma's suspicious eyes.

That night, as soon as he hit the bed, Nnamdi fell fast asleep. But again it wasn't a peaceful sleep. For what felt like hours, he was chased by the shadowy grotesque demon version of Three Days' Journey, who seemed to be made of a sticky brown goop that stained everything it touched. And always present was the glowing Ikenga, now the size of his father, floating after him and pointing its machete.

Nnamdi opened his eyes and the dreams instantly shrunk away. This dream seemed far less serious than the one he'd had the first night he'd changed. He shook his head, rubbed his face, and looked outside. Still night. He sat up and picked up the Ikenga. The strange electrical charge coming from it no longer really hurt. Instead, it felt like a force making his hand do what he didn't tell it to do. The Ikenga was still warm. He turned it over, feeling the charge softly thrum in his fingertips. What would happen if he threw the thing in the garbage? Would he stop changing? He didn't want to throw it away, though; it was a gift from his father, a gift his father could only give or not give, with no advice.

He focused his eyes on it. Then he strained with all his might to intentionally bring forth his shadow body. He thought about the feeling of being big. Being powerful. Being black like the moonless night. He imagined he could hear a pin drop from ten houses away. That he could smell a drop of gasoline leaking from the generator next door. That he could feel the slightest shift in the air as someone walked by outside.

What if he could teach himself to *control* it? Then he could be a mighty force in Kaleria. He could be his father 2.0. Maybe this was why his father had even given it to him, to make him Nnamdi, the young son of the town's greatest police chief, who had finished what his father started. He'd be like Batman. *Yes*, he thought. *I could teach myself to control it.*

It would all make sense. "Oh, let's give it a try," he whispered. He took a deep breath. "Okay, here goes."

Nnamdi held his breath and imagined he was wrestling a great shadowy beast. He strained until his head ached, trying to squeeze the beast within him into a shape he could control. He felt it move within him and then fall on top of him, knocking the breath from his chest. "Ooof!" he grunted. He gathered himself and tried again. Then again. Then again. Breathless, he lay back on his bed. He stayed that way for an hour, thinking and thinking. Eventually, he fell asleep. He had not one dream.

7

Untruth

"A BAD DAY for Bad Market," the newsletter headline shouted.

"I'll read it when I get home," Nnamdi muttered to himself, handing naira to the seller, folding the newsletter under his arm, and walking away from the newsstand. It was Saturday morning and people were taking advantage of the pleasant cooler weather. Some sat outside their homes, playing cards and sipping from cold bottles of beer. The woman who sold akara was already preparing her frying pan, small fire, and oil to fry the tasty bean cakes she'd sell that afternoon.

"Good morning, Mrs. Abassi," Nnamdi said.

She smiled. "Good morning, Nnamdi." He'd known Mrs. Abassi since he could remember. His father loved her akara and would buy from her several times a week. She was a smart old lady, especially when it came to math. Nnamdi and Chioma often came to her for help with homework when she wasn't busy. "Is that today's paper?" she asked.

"Yes," he said.

"Read that one myself," she said. "Bad Market, what a waste of a young man. But who do you suppose this so-called shadow man is? He must be really black. Maybe he is a yam farmer who is sick of Kaleria's problems."

Nnamdi shrugged, avoiding her eyes.

"Doesn't matter to me, either," she said. "As long as he sticks around. A man like that, we need him here."

When Nnamdi got back, his mother was in the kitchen, preparing a breakfast of pap with a bit of sugar and condensed milk as she quietly talked on the phone. *She's in a good mood,* Nnamdi thought. She turned her back to Nnamdi so that he couldn't quite hear what she was saying and Nnamdi glanced curiously at her for a moment. However, he had other more pressing concerns and he quickly turned his attention to the paper. He sat at the table and unfolded it, a frown on his face. The story's headline bothered him when he read it a second time. "A Bad Day for Bad Market" sounded almost sympathetic to Bad Market's plight. That couldn't be right.

His mother giggled as she stirred Nnamdi's pap. He looked up and frowned more deeply. Who was she talking to? When she didn't look back, he sighed, returning his attention to his newsletter. His father used to buy the newsletter every morning, too. Reading it from beginning to end was his first activity each day. Nnamdi began to read.

Yesterday, in broad daylight, one of Kaleria's greatest nuisances was assaulted. "I was sure he was going to kill me," a tearful and beaten Bad Market said. He explained that after he had robbed the market, the mysterious man had snatched him up and beaten him bloody. He said his life would have surely been over if it hadn't been for people coming to see what was happening. . . .

His mother placed his bowl of pap before him and he barely noticed. "This can't be right," Nnamdi whispered. His mother left the kitchen and he was glad. He couldn't have hidden the disgust on his face. The worst part came a few paragraphs later. The new chief of police, who'd been sworn in three months after his father's death, took advantage of the moment to make a strong statement—a statement that included a photo.

Concerning the incident, Chief of Police Ojini Okimba laid down the law. "We don't know who this mysterious wannabe vigilante is," Chief Okimba said. "He makes no effort to give a statement at the police department. He leaves no letter. He tells nothing to anyone. All we know is that he is a big, tall dark-skinned man. So I will call him that. The Man. And listen to me well when I say that the Man is a MENACE TO SOCIETY and should be treated as such. There is no room for primitive irresponsible 'jungle justice' in my civilized town. We are making every effort to arrest the Man and bring him to proper justice like every other criminal."

On the front page was a photo of Chief Okimba looking strong and confident in his expensive suit. Nnamdi bristled. He hadn't liked Chief Okimba since his father's funeral, where the man had given a speech that subtly blamed Nnamdi's father for his own death. Okimba said that Nnamdi's father was probably too hard on criminals and too good a man for his job. Nnamdi remembered the exact words in Okimba's speech that had really angered him: "In his next life, such a fine police officer will know better."

There had been frowning, grumbling, and forced applause afterward. No one knew if Okimba was complimenting or insulting Nnamdi's father. But Nnamdi's mother wasn't confused at all. She knew Chief Okimba was insulting Nnamdi's father's efforts and she was seething with anger. Nnamdi had followed her into the kitchen for a few minutes, where his mother wept and cursed Okimba. He remembered looking out the window, facing the event tent where everyone was gathered, and seeing Chief Okimba shamelessly posing for pictures near the open casket.

The next day, those very pictures were on the front page of the *Kaleria Sun*. The caption read, "In Comes Okimba, the Gentle Giant to Stamp Crime Out with Flash and Dash."

And now here was Okimba doing and saying stupid things again. What Nnamdi had done was not "jungle justice," not really. It certainly wasn't "irresponsible." What about the drunk driver who was lynched in the streets months ago? His burned-up vehicle remained on the side of the road, serving as a warning for possible future drunk drivers! Chief Okimba was still silent on that incident. Now Chief Okimba, who was known for taking bribes himself, was urging Kaleria's citizens to be vigilant. And worst of all, according to the newsletter, he was offering a small reward for any information about the identity and whereabouts of "the Man."

On the third page, where the story continued, there was a photo of Bad Market looking pathetic and unconscious on the ground. He was tied with the scarf and his mouth was open, saliva dribbling from the side. Nnamdi took one look at the ridiculous photo and, despite himself, burst out laughing.

There was a knock at the door and Nnamdi immediately quieted. The sound reminded him of the night his father died, when he'd opened the door and found the envelope containing that letter. But it was morning. And the knock was fast and light. Chioma.

"I'll get it," Nnamdi called, getting up.

Chioma wore jeans and a T-shirt, had a hand on her hip and an inquisitive look on her face. "Good morning, Nnamdi," she said. "My mum is soaking stockfish and *mangala* fish. The house stinks like crazy. What is it with bad smells? First Bad Market and now this!" Chioma had a sensitive nose and was always complaining about various smells. She said this was why she would never live in Lagos. She always left the house and came over when her mother was soaking dried fish.

Nnamdi laughed. "Come on, then," he said. "I'll take you where it smells like flowers."

She grinned and they went around back to the garden. Nnamdi knelt down to touch the delicate leaves of the yam vine as Chioma slowly walked through the garden. In a matter of days, the vine had grown so much.

"You did all this?" Chioma asked, poking at a fattening tomato.

Nnamdi only smiled. His father had planted the garden. The foundation had been laid years before Nnamdi was even born. "It's Daddy's garden, always has been."

"Oh, you know what I mean," Chioma said.

Nnamdi shrugged.

"What did you plant here?" she asked, pointing to the bare patch. There had been some roses there, but they had died during the year of neglect.

Nnamdi looked at the yam vine and couldn't keep the smile from his lips when he said, "Your sunflower seeds."

Chioma squealed with delight. "Really?! *Finally!* I'm so glad!"

"Oh, calm down," he quickly said with a soft laugh. "Sunflowers need a lot of care. I don't know if they will grow."

But Chioma only stared at the spot and grinned, and Nnamdi knew she'd blocked out his negativity. Sunflowers were her "favorite, favorite, favoritest flower on earth." He'd known that when he planted them and he'd known she'd nearly die with happiness when he told her.

"I'm going to come by every day until they are huge flowery suns!" she announced. "I'll help you water them."

Nnamdi just laughed. Chioma was so predictable.

"Nnamdi . . ." She paused, looking back at the house. He could hear his mother talking on the phone. "Come walk with me," she said, lowering her voice. "I want to ask you something."

"Okay," he slowly said, hoping it wasn't anything difficult to explain.

After telling his mother where they were going, they quickly walked around the house to the front.

"Did you see the newsletter?" Chioma asked. They waved to Mr. Oke as they slipped through the open gate.

"Yeah."

"Daddy nearly choked on his bread, reading it this morning," she said. She snorted. "Did you see that picture of Bad Market?"

"He deserved to be shown like that," Nnamdi said.

She nodded. "Bad Market once robbed my aunt of a month's worth of rent money. He might be good-looking, but he's dangerous. So why did the newsletter make him look harmless?"

"No idea. But at least he's off the street," he said. "'The Man' made sure of that. The article said he's in the hospital, being watched by police."

"'The Man,'" she spat. "Who is this 'Man'? If people start doing whatever they want, there won't be any order around here. He's worse than the criminals!"

"You must be joking!" Nnamdi said, taken aback.

"You could have been hurt yesterday," she suddenly said, stopping and turning to him. They were standing under a wide mango tree. Chioma reached up and angrily plucked a leaf and pointed at him with it. "Why'd you go running into the market like that?"

"Chioma, let's just relax and enjoy the morning."

She put her arms over her chest and squinted at him, looking more suspicious than ever. Behind them, cars and trucks zoomed by on the road. She pushed a braid out of her face and cocked her head. "What *happened* yesterday, Nnamdi? What did you see?"

"I saw what . . . I saw what you saw," he stammered.

"How? Your mother and I weren't in that stinking stench. We went in when it cleared. And . . . and you couldn't have seen what I saw; you weren't there. You'd have told me."

"What . . ." Nnamdi paused, then he scoffed. "I don't want to talk about it." He hated lying and, really, what was he supposed to tell her? The truth? That he could turn into some super-strong giant shadow man because of an Ikenga his ghost father had given him? He wished she'd just shut up and stop trying to make him lie.

"I think you're—"

Nnamdi felt his temper suddenly rise sharply. He flared his nostrils and stepped closer to her. She didn't budge. "Why are you always shouting at me?" he said. "You always think I'm doing something wrong!"

"I'm not shouting," she said. She shook her head. "I didn't . . ."

"Didn't what?" he shouted. He stepped closer. This time, she frowned and stepped back. "What kind of friend are you? All I did was go in there and try to help and you're acting like I . . . I robbed someone!"

The corners of her eyes quivered as she fought back tears. "You did *something*. I know it!" she shouted into his face. This time, tears did escape. "Something's going on! And you're hiding it!"

Rage hit him so hard and suddenly that he shuddered. He saw red and felt his body flare hot. His mouth tasted metallic. His mind went blank and his body felt as if a demon had taken it over. He balled his fists, lunging at her, his arm raised to strike. Chioma jumped back, staring at him, appalled. Two women passing by stopped. "What are you doing?" one of the women shouted, running over and grabbing his arm.

Just as suddenly as it happened, Nnamdi came back to himself. His body relaxed and he literally felt himself shrink three inches. Chioma sobbed, still staring at him in shock. Then she turned and ran off. The woman holding his arm stared at him, astonished.

"I'm sorry," he muttered.

"What kind of child are you?" the woman snapped.

"Acting like an animal," the other woman said. "Shameful."

"Never, *ever* hit a woman or a *girl!*" the first woman said, pointing a finger in his face and then giving his forehead a hard shove. "*Tufiakwa!* God forbid!"

"Sorry," Nnamdi whispered, stepping away from the women. "I'm so sorry. I . . . I wasn't myself." He quickly walked in the other direction before the women could say anything more.

He was glad when the women didn't pursue him. He walked and walked and his legs took him to where he liked to go when he needed to think: the old abandoned school down the road, past his own school, past the market, on Kosisochukwu Road, beyond the patch of bush. It was quiet here, and only palm-wine tappers or men hunting for the occasional bumbling grasscutter came here these days.

He'd run here the morning after he found out his father had been killed. He'd stayed there all day, sitting at an old desk and staring at the wall. He'd worried his mother sick. She hadn't known that he liked to come here, so she hadn't known where to look other than at Chioma's house. When he wasn't there, Chioma's mother had had to catch

Nnamdi's mother as she fell to the floor, distraught. When Nnamdi came home later that day, she'd beaten him and then hugged him close. Even then, he hadn't told his mother exactly where he'd been; all he'd said was that he'd gone for a long walk.

Now Nnamdi walked past the unfinished wall that was supposed to be built around the school. He was still quivering with shame and . . . rage. So much so that he was probably walking unsteadily, like someone trying to walk as the earth shook. There was a rough-barked tree growing there and he punched it with a fist as he passed. He stopped, backtracked, and stared at the trunk, then at his normal-sized fist, then back at the tree. The dent in it was deep. His fist had made that. Leaves fell from the tree's branches.

He shuddered again, seeing Three Days' Journey flying back like a rag doll when he'd slapped him. Nnamdi had heard he had a broken jaw. And now he'd nearly hit Chioma. He could have *killed* her if he'd done that. "What is wrong with me?" he moaned. "What's it doing to me? Do Ikengas have side effects? Maybe its powers are poisoning me." He touched the dent in the tree. "Sorry," he whispered. "Sorry." He didn't want to voice what he suspected deep in his heart . . . that the rage had nothing to do with the Ikenga and the powers it gave him, that the rage was *his own*. Rage at his father being murdered, his murder remaining unsolved, his mother's suffering, his town slowly being overrun by the criminals his father had died trying to stop.

Before all this, he'd never even gotten into a fistfight at school. The worst rage he felt was when he was reading about characters like the Hulk and Wolverine. "Sorry," he said one more time to the tree. Not knowing what else to do, he walked into the concrete building, sat on the cool floor, and gazed at the wall.

8

Glares and Stares

THE NEXT DAY, if Chioma stopped by to water the sunflower seeds, Nnamdi didn't see her do it. He didn't see her on the way to school or in the schoolyard. When he finally saw her during lunchtime, Nnamdi softly tapped Chioma's shoulder. "Chioma," he said, keeping his voice low so his classmates wouldn't hear. "I'm sorry. I don't know what came over me. I think I was tired . . . or something."

She turned to him, her eyes full of rage. She kept walking, showing her back to him as she hiked up her backpack and joined her group of friends.

Stung, Nnamdi quickly turned away and walked over to Ruff Diamond, Hassan, and Jide, who were playing nails in the box. Nnamdi watched as his friends drew boxes on the sand and competed to see who could dig the most nails in each box without the nails falling. Too preoccupied to pay attention, Nnamdi sat on the grass a few feet away and wrapped his arms around his legs as he watched Chioma chat animatedly with her friend Onuchi. She laughed as Onuchi showed her something on her cell phone, but every so often she'd glare directly at Nnamdi. He'd glare right back until she'd toss her braids and look away. He looked at his feet, his belly rolling with guilt. He wished he knew how to convince her he was sorry. But why did she have to make it so hard?

By the time all the kids spilled into the schoolyard on their way home, Nnamdi could barely contain his anger. All day, he'd seemed to be looking at Chioma's back. In the hallway, during class, during recess, and now as school let out. As he stood with his friends, he watched Chioma and her girlfriends buy Fanta and Coca-Cola from a hawker on the side of the road. He knew she'd buy Bitter Lemon, her favorite.

"I think if we gang up on him, he'll lower the price," Jide was saying. Jide, Hassan, and Ruff Diamond were about to accost the bun-seller for having the nerve to raise his prices this week.

"The man is stubborn," Hassan said. "He'll probably raise the prices even more if we do that. He knows he's the only one around here who sells them."

"And it's not the price, man," Ruff Diamond said. "It's the size. Who wants to eat those bite-sized things he's switched to selling?"

Nnamdi couldn't have cared less. He gazed at Chioma.

How could he have raised a hand to his friend . . . his best friend? He had his school buddies, sure. They played soccer after school and talked about girls. But Chioma was the only person who noticed how quiet he'd gotten after his father's death. She was the only one who asked him why he liked pepper soup with fish in it instead of goat meat. She was the only one who'd known his father as well as he had.

"Hey! Nnamdi?!"

He nearly jumped, taking his eyes from Chioma to glare at his friend Jide. He could feel a headache coming on. "What, Jide?" Nnamdi snapped. But he couldn't help it. He glanced back at Chioma one more time. "What is it?"

Jide laughed loudly. "What is it with you and that girl Chioma?"

Ruff Diamond snickered. "Isn't it obvious? She dumped him!"

"HA HA!" Jide shouted. "You must be kidding. You *dated* her? That rascally looking loudmouthed girl? I thought she was just your neighbor or family friend."

Nnamdi could barely contain himself. His headache was raging, and he felt his muscles tense up.

Ruff Diamond chuckled lightheartedly. "If you get her to date you again, you should ask her to wash her crazy hair."

"Shut up," Nnamdi said through clenched teeth. "Do I need to mention Fisayo dumping you because of your body odor?"

The smile dropped from Ruff Diamond's face. "Look at this idiot," Ruff Diamond said to Jide. Hassan had long since backed away, seeming to sense things were about to get bad. "Who are you?" Ruff Diamond hissed, looking Nnamdi up and down. Jide laughed, siding with Ruff Diamond, and Ruff Diamond kept talking. "They kill your father in his own office, yet some shadow guy comes and takes out two of those criminals in two nights. He did in two days what your father couldn't do in *years!* You come from weak stock, man."

POW! Nnamdi punched Ruff Diamond in the face before he knew what he was doing. He felt his fist connect with Ruff Diamond's chin. Ruff Diamond was a tall, strong boy, much bigger than Nnamdi. But to Nnamdi right now, Ruff Diamond was nothing. Ruff Diamond stumbled, then lunged at Nnamdi, bringing his fist back. Nnamdi easily stepped aside and pushed him down.

"Gonna kill you!" Ruff Diamond growled, trying to get to his feet, sniffing back tears.

Nnamdi kicked him back down. "Stay down!" Nnamdi roared, his voice deepening. He was shaking now. Ruff Diamond whimpered, went flat on the ground, and did not move. Jide and Hassan stood feet away, shocked. "Stay in the dirt where you belong!" Nnamdi said. "You cover yourself with all that bling, but underneath you're just like everyone else." He looked up and met Chioma's eyes and immediately his clouded mind cleared. *My voice*, he realized. *Oh God! What am I doing?!* He felt himself deflate. Had he grown taller, too?

". . . hurting him!" she was saying. She'd been standing there all along, shouting at him. "STOP IT!" Her friend Onuchi stood behind her, grabbing at her arm and staring at Nnamdi with terrified eyes.

"Leave him," Onuchi screeched. "He's crazy!"

THUMP THUMP. The pounding was deep in his head. *THUMP THUMP.* And it seemed as if a red shadow lifted from his eyes. *THUMP THUMP.* Nnamdi just stood there as Chioma helped Ruff Diamond up. His nose was bleeding and his face was swollen. Nnamdi looked around. Hassan, Jide, and several other kids stood around him, silent, eyes wide.

"What's wrong with you, Nnamdi?" Chioma shouted at him. Nnamdi glared at her, ignoring a pang of guilt. All day she had refused to speak to him and now, finally, after he'd nearly killed one of his stupid friends, she decided to say something. Nnamdi wiped the tears of anger from his eyes, shoved his hands in his pockets, and quickly walked away.

He saw that Chioma let her friend pull her away in the opposite direction. *Good,* he thought. He didn't want to be around anyone. His vision had gone red and black when he was beating his friend. He could feel the size and strength of the Man within him, powering his punches, fueling his rage. What was happening to him?

He pushed the image of Ruff Diamond's bloody face out

of his mind. He had done that. Car horns blasted at him as he walked onto the road, not looking to see if any cars were coming. He didn't care. *I should throw the Ikenga away*, he thought. But throwing it away would make him feel more hopeless. No, he'd do no such thing. It wasn't the Ikenga's fault. *Ruff Diamond had it coming*, he thought darkly.

"Good afternoon," Mr. Oke said, opening the gate for him.

"Afternoon," Nnamdi muttered, looking down so that Mr. Oke wouldn't see his red swollen eyes. He'd tried to hold them back, but as he walked home, the tears kept coming.

Mr. Oke walked up to him. "What's wrong? You look—"

"I'm fine," he said, quickly moving past him. He wasn't ready for any questions. Not yet. His mother would hear about the fight by the end of the day anyway. Nnamdi froze. There was a blue Mercedes parked in the driveway, right in front of the house. Nnamdi frowned.

"Nnamdi, did someone hurt you?" Mr. Oke asked.

Nnamdi just shook his head. Mr. Oke's cell phone went off and he held up a hand as he answered it. He grinned widely, "Vicky," he said. "Baby, I've been waiting for your call." He walked away for privacy and Nnamdi quickly went inside. He entered the living room and froze.

His mother was sitting on the couch. "Nnamdi, honey," she said. A man sat on the couch as well and he was seated way too close to her. She quickly got up, pausing for a moment to look at his dirty school uniform. "Nnamdi, this is my friend Mr. Bonny Chibuzor."

The man stood and stepped up to Nnamdi.

"Nice to meet you," he said, shaking Nnamdi's hand firmly.

Mr. Bonny Chibuzor was not as tall as Nnamdi's father. But he was built strong. He looked like one of those construction workers who lifted and cemented concrete blocks all day. The only difference was that he wore a stylish suit and his big hands were not that rough.

"Your mother has told me many good things about you," Bonny added.

"Well, she hasn't told me anything about you," Nnamdi said.

"Nnamdi!" his mother snapped. Then she chuckled. "He's just tired from school." She gave Nnamdi a dirty look.

"It's nice to meet you, sir," Nnamdi said, lowering his head. He glanced at his mother. "Can I go do my homework?"

"Please do," his mother coolly said.

9

The Go-Slow

IT TOOK NNAMDI two weeks to accept it; his mother was dating Bonny. Nnamdi had to see him every Saturday and many times during the week, when Bonny would drive his mother to and from the market. Bonny, who was a medical doctor, always had a smile on his face and something in his hands that made his mother squeal with delight. His mother had settled into the job selling tapioca and now even had a stall in the market. Nnamdi's mother had her pride, so she refused when Bonny offered to help with money.

She didn't even let Bonny help with Nnamdi's school fees or groceries. However, she enjoyed the little things he bought her—like fresh fish, delicious teas, and a dress he knew she had her eye on. Nnamdi had never seen his mother like this and he wasn't sure whether it relieved or irritated him. He didn't like Bonny, no matter how many packets of biscuits he gave Nnamdi or how many times he asked how school was going.

Bonny had recently bought his mother her first cell phone. His father had never liked cell phones and banned them from the house. His mother had not argued about this, despite the fact that all her friends had them. Nnamdi wondered if this had to do with the fact that his mother never wanted to receive the News on her cell. But not owning a phone hadn't kept away the News that every family of a police officer dreads. Nnamdi had received the Letter instead. Maybe the fact that she'd gotten the News regardless was why she accepted the cell phone from Bonny.

Nnamdi hated hearing his mother chat with Bonny in the evenings. The sound of his mother's happy voice made him think about his father and the fact that he wasn't there. The only direct connection he had to his father now was the Ikenga. The Ikenga! What to do with it? He wished he could ask Chioma what he should do, but it had been two weeks now and Chioma was still not speaking to him. Neither were any of his friends.

Nnamdi sighed as he stared out the car window, his mind heavy with his own miseries and confusion. He still had no idea how to control when he changed into the Man. It hadn't happened since that time with Bad Market. And he still had not gotten revenge on the Chief of Chiefs. His world was upside down and now he was in Bonny's car with his mother on their way to eat at the Calabar Kitchen Restaurant.

"I'm not kidding, o," Bonny was saying to Nnamdi's mother. She laughed hard and tapped him on the shoulder to stop talking. But he kept going. "The woman was so empty-headed that when she finally got to the house, she forgot her child in the car, and the taxi driver . . ." Both he and Nnamdi's mother totally lost it, laughing like crazy. Nnamdi hoped Bonny wouldn't crash his precious blue Mercedes. But then again, *that* would be kind of funny. The only time Bonny had ever gotten irritated with Nnamdi was when he saw Nnamdi leaning against the vehicle one day.

"Off the car!" he'd snapped, coming out of the house.

When Nnamdi had quickly moved away, Bonny had polished the place Nnamdi had been touching, using the sleeve of his white shirt. *Bonny would probably have a heart attack if he ever crashed his car,* Nnamdi thought. Of course, that wasn't likely to happen today, as they'd just gotten stuck in a "go-slow." Who knew how long they'd be in the congested traffic?

Sunset was fast approaching and Nnamdi's stomach was growling. He had his mother's cell phone and was playing Connect Four on it to keep himself occupied. He was winning. His mother let out another peal of laughter and Nnamdi squeezed her phone in anger. *CRACK!* He gasped. He'd crushed it. A piece of plastic fell to the floor.

He stared at the phone, feeling a drop in the pit of his belly. His mother was going to kill him. And how was he going to explain how he did it? In the car? He looked at his mother and Bonny and wondered if he should say something now while they were both in such a giggly mood. A shadow passed his window and he felt a chill.

"Mommy, did you see that?" he asked.

But she and Bonny were fiddling with the radio. Bonny found a music station and she shimmied her shoulders as Bonny sang along to the tune. The windows were down and the car's engine was off, the same as the other vehicles around them. Nnamdi leaned out the window to see if he could spot anything ahead. There were hawkers walking from window to window, selling peanuts, plantain chips, "pure water," and Coca-Cola. Things seemed normal enough. But he could feel it in his chest—something was very wrong.

He was looking through the windshield when he saw his mother's purse disappear right before his eyes. He blinked. It had been there. Sitting on the dashboard. Then it was gone!

"Mommy!" he shouted, pointing to where her purse had been. "Your purse!"

She frowned a bit at him, looking annoyed at being shaken from her enjoyment of the music.

"Eh?" Bonny asked.

"Mommy's purse!" Nnamdi insisted. "It was right there! It's gone! I saw it disappear!"

His mother started, looking around her seat. "Oh my God," she said. "Oh my God!" Bonny started looking around his seat, too.

He felt the softest touch in his hand. He looked down.

Now the crushed mobile phone was gone! He was about to say something when Bonny jumped up, bashing his head on the car ceiling. "Ah!" he exclaimed, rubbing his head. He started looking around like crazy. "My watch, o! What is going on?"

Nnamdi heard similar exclamations from other vehicles all around him. People's things were disappearing left and right. Some people jumped out of their cars and ran off.

"It's Mama Go-Slow!" his mother said, taking off her seat belt. "We need to get out of here immediately. Sometimes she has people beaten. She won't take the car; that's not how she operates."

Nnamdi looked around, his body tingly with adrenaline. He knew what he was going to do. All he had to do was *do* it. *I can do it*, he thought. He remembered what Mama Go-Slow looked like at the funeral—wearing her stylish red abada clothing and blocky black shoes as she walked like a buffalo. She was a scary lady.

"You sure they won't take my car?!" Bonny said, looking distressed.

"Yes, yes," his mother said, jumping out of the car. "My . . . my husband said she never steals cars. Just people's things." She opened Nnamdi's door. "Come on! Move, move, move!"

Nnamdi got out and ran down the road behind his mother and Bonny and everyone else. When they weren't watching, he stopped beside a truck. His legs felt rubbery. He looked at his mother and Bonny as they ran farther and farther, thinking he was right behind them. He bit his lip, his heart slamming in his chest. "Go," he said. But he couldn't move. "Go! Go, Nnamdi!" he shouted, and ran to the other side of the truck. He got down and rolled beneath it. He waited. Only for a moment. He gasped as he felt himself change into the Man. Everything stretched and he was sure he could crush bricks with his bare hands. This time it felt nearly voluntary and with the change came something else. His uneasiness disappeared. "Where is she?" he whispered to himself in his low, rumbly voice. He waited some more.

From under the truck, he saw feet run by. Gym shoes. Sandals. Slippers. Pumps. Flip-flops. Oxfords. Big and small. All running. Then he saw a pair of wide, chunky black shoes standing a few cars away. He leaned out a bit and could see the shoes belonged to a pair of short, fat legs. He rolled out and jumped up.

She had her back to Nnamdi and he stared at her. She was a short, stocky woman with patchy fair brown skin and thick, bushy black eyebrows. His father had speculated that she colored them with coal to make herself look more intimidating. Today she wore a bright yellow dress that barely reached her knees. Her method of attack was to wait until traffic was heavy and people got comfortable and turned off their vehicles. Then she and her trained thugs would descend on the cars, SUVs, and trucks, robbing people of everything they had with them . . . including useless things like crushed cell phones. Mama Go-Slow was a trained *dibia* gifted in the arts of all kinds of juju and charms, a ninja and an expert in the South African martial art of Musangwe. His father had said she taught her thugs the art of blending in and fighting, so that, like ninjas, they were not seen or heard when they struck, and like Musangwe fighters, you did not want to cross them.

Nnamdi hid behind a car, mere yards from Mama Go-Slow. He watched her as she proudly observed her thugs do her work. She laughed crazily as people ran for their lives. A few of her thugs, who were dressed in camouflage bodysuits and were probably older teenage boys, purposely knocked people over and shouted and slapped at them until they fled.

"Yes, yes, panic," Mama Go-Slow loudly said. "Run. This road has a toll you must pay. I am like the troll under the bridge: pay me or you can't pass." She laughed heartily, her round belly vibrating.

Nnamdi took a deep breath; watching her like this gave him such a bad, bad feeling. It was now or never. He ran at her like a great lumbering black beast. If he grabbed her quickly enough, he could get a hand over her mouth and drag her away from the road before her thugs spotted them. *But she's just a tiny old woman,* he briefly thought. He pushed the thought away. None of her thugs were around her. He would grab the collar of her dress and . . . She turned to him just before he reached her. *WHAM!* As if he'd run into a wall! He stumbled back and sat down hard, dazed. Right there on the road.

Mama Go-Slow belly-laughed heartily as Nnamdi shook his head and pushed himself up, reaching out again to grab her, harnessing all his super-strength. The invisible force slammed into him again and he fell back to the street. This time the force ground his face onto the warm concrete. He painfully twisted his neck, fighting to keep his eye on her.

"And stay down," she said, still laughing.

"Mama, are you all right?" one of her helpers asked her as he ran up. He was carrying several purses.

"Oh, I'm fine," she said, gazing down her nose at Nnamdi. "Gather the others. Have them take everything to the car. This is the Man and I'm going to show him who *really* has the power."

The boy looked down at Nnamdi with wide eyes. He shuddered and took a step away. "That's . . . ?"

"Yes," she snapped. "Don't get distracted. Finish the job. I will finish *him*." She laughed loudly. "Today is a good day."

Nnamdi wanted to get up, but the pain, oh the pain. *So evil*, he angrily thought. *Thief!* For the first time, Nnamdi really, truly, deeply understood why his father risked his life to get rid of people like this woman. *Laughing like a wild animal as she takes people's hard-earned things.* A surge of righteous fury flooded into Nnamdi and he felt as if he were dunked in hot water. More pain. But this pain energized him and his world turned red.

He started to get up.

"Stay DOWN," Mama Go-Slow said again. This time, she strained as she used her strange juju on him. When he fell back down, she smiled triumphantly, slightly out of breath. "Temper, temper, young man. Resistance is futile."

She leaned closer to him. She smelled heavily of perfume and he could see that she had several flower-shaped rings on her stubby fingers. She brought her face so close that he could smell her sour minty breath. He frowned as she looked into his eyes. Her eyebrows went up with surprise. She grinned. "Oh, this is rich," she said. She brought her face closer. "Who gave you the juju, boy? This is quite a costume."

Nnamdi was so shocked, he nearly forgot how to breathe.

She cackled and said, "I seeee you. Son of the dead Chief Icheteka. Did you know I had my kids sneak into your house and steal from it during your father's funeral? Nothing big or important. Just . . . things. Did you notice? Or just feel *something* wasn't right?" She smiled, showing all of her teeth. "Your father was a real thorn in my side. I'm glad the Chief of Chiefs did away with him."

Nnamdi's vision went black for a moment. When it returned, he was still seeing red. His heart was slamming in his chest.

"I took that glass apple myself and *smashed* it to pieces on the ground." She laughed hard.

Nnamdi's angry eyes fell on her blocky shoes and then on her smug, smirking face. Her smirk turned to a grin as she brought back her shoe and kicked Nnamdi hard in the side. Nnamdi moaned. Whether he was the Man or not, he felt every inch of the kick. He tried with all his might to get up, fight back. She kicked him in the gut again. "I said, stay *down.*"

She kicked him again and again and again, laughing. "The Man, indeed," she said. *Kick!* "What does it turn you into?" *Kick!* "A ghost?" *Kick!* "A masked man?" *Kick!* "You're just a little boy. You will never be mightier than me." *Kick!*

Nnamdi could barely breathe, the pain was so terrible. Stars bounced and exploded before his eyes and then the world started to go black again. He was slipping into unconsciousness. Slipping. Slipping.

BANG!

He was jarred alert by the loud sound of the gunshot. There was a flash of yellow-white light. A pain in his chest. Then another *BANG!* More pain, this coming from his neck. He was in his father's office. He was his father on the day he was shot. *Daddy was shot in the neck, too,* Nnamdi realized. He was falling. He saw his mother's face glowing like the rising sun. He saw his own face, bathed in sunshine. Then he saw Kaleria, clean and brilliant.

Nnamdi shut his eyes, a sob deep in his chest. "Daddy," he whispered. "I won't let you down."

"Nnamdi," he heard his father say. Nnamdi opened his eyes. He'd just felt his father's pain from when he was shot. Shot twice. Now he felt his own pain from Mama Go-Slow's beating. Realization, understanding, and fresh rage rippled through him like an electric shock. "No!" he shouted, feeling every one of his powerful strange muscles flex. He fought his way to his feet, despite the fact that she tried to press him back down. Who was she? She may have been powerful, but his father had come from death and given him an Ikenga. An Ikenga from a father who had vowed to do good. An Ikenga given with love, hope, and dreams. He was protected. Nnamdi had forgotten. Now he remembered. He had a task to do.

When Nnamdi stood up tall, so very tall, the smug smile dropped from Mama Go-Slow's face. Nnamdi's mind was clear now and he locked eyes with her. "Come on," Nnamdi growled. "Try something else on me." She contemplated him for another moment and reached into her pockets. When she brought her hands out, they were covered in something that looked like sparkling blue glitter. However, when she looked up at Nnamdi, she froze.

"I'm waiting," Nnamdi growled. "Come on."

She paused. Then she turned and ran. Nnamdi was faster. He snatched the collar of her dress.

"What kind of man are you?" she shouted, exaggeratedly struggling and groaning. The glittery stuff flew and then fled from her hands like terrified flies. "Is this how you treat your elders?!"

"When they are criminals, yes," Nnamdi said, dragging her to one of the cars. "And I am not a man. I'm a boy!" He was glad to see the door was open. He could still feel the pain from her beating and it cleared his head and kept sympathy away. He shoved her into the car and then walked around it, breaking the latches so that she couldn't escape.

When he was done, he gazed in at her. She gazed back and frowned. "You play with fire, boy," she said, cocking her head. No longer looking so helpless. "Juju takes as much as it gives. No matter who takes it."

"You are done," was all Nnamdi said. "If you try to get out, I will know and I will come and smash you more than you smashed me, I swear it." As he walked away, he felt anything but triumphant. He felt like crying.

Nnamdi waited nearby, hiding behind a car and watching. Mama Go-Slow sat angrily, looking out the window the entire time. Not once did she try to get out. *Like a snake,* Nnamdi thought as he watched. *She's so smart that she even knows when she can't win. I'll bet she even knows I'm watching; that's why she's not trying to escape.* Then he spotted some police coming along and checking cars. He shouted, "Look in that car! Mama Go-Slow is trapped in it!" Nnamdi took off when he saw that the car was surrounded by police, some pointing their guns as two officers worked to open the door.

He was inside Bonny's car minutes later. He'd changed back before he even stepped inside; it was like the power came when he needed it and left when he didn't. It took Bonny and his mother nearly a half hour to return. The alone time helped him get his head together and put on an indifferent face. His body ached horribly from the beating. When Bonny and his mother returned to the car, he explained away his dirty clothes by saying he'd gotten knocked down in the rush. He didn't have to explain his mother's broken cell phone. He hated lying, but these days he was full of lies. The police had Mama Go-Slow, but her thugs had escaped with their stolen items.

Because neither Bonny nor his mother had any money on them anymore, they simply drove back and spent a quiet evening at home. Neither of them complained when Nnamdi retired early to his room. As he inspected his body in the mirror, he found deep bruises on his sides and some scratches on his arms, chest, and knees. They ached and stung so much that he knew it would be hard to keep them from his mother. Thankfully, this was the extent of it. So his guise as the Man protected him from severe harm. This was good information to know.

10

Popcorn

Yesterday, after conducting a mass robbery on the evening traffic of Ochulor Street, Ekwedigwe Tumtumbroni Babatunde, better known as Mama Go-Slow, was severely beaten up by the Man right in the middle of the road. Babatunde is 80 years old and says that sometimes she must walk with a cane. "He was like an animal," Babatunde said. "I'm just an old woman. Was the violence necessary?" She had to be carried to her jail cell, where a doctor was brought in to see to her injuries.

"The woman is mentally unstable," the doctor who saw to her said. "The Man beat her black and blue and then shoved and locked her in a car on a suffocatingly hot evening. He should be ashamed of himself!"

Although the Man is responsible for the capture

*of the infamous Mama Go-Slow, police officials,
including the chief of police, continue to stress that the
Man is a menace to society. "He is a serious threat to
the well-being of Kaleria," Chief Ojini Okimba said.
"We are doing all we can, but I suggest that, until
we apprehend him, Kaleria citizens should avoid being
out after dark and keep their doors locked and secure."
The reward for the Man's capture or information
about his identity or whereabouts has been raised to
7 million naira.*

Nnamdi angrily crumpled the paper up as he walked to
school. His muscles still ached from yesterday's thrashing. He
couldn't quite bend his left arm because of a bruise there.
Unnecessary violence, indeed.

He shoved the balled-up newsletter into his backpack and
kept walking. Everyone he passed had a copy and was either
reading it or carrying it and discussing what they had heard
with someone else. He even saw a man reading while driving. He passed a stall selling newsletters and there wasn't one
copy left. The woman sitting on a stool beside the stall was
in an especially chipper mood.

"Good morning," she said, smiling at Nnamdi.

"Good morning." Of course she was happy; she'd made
a small fortune selling all those newsletters. A newsletter full of huge wild lies. Everyone was being misinformed!

How could anyone believe Mama Go-Slow was this weak old woman? Didn't people have any memory? Still, people wanted to know when and where the Man would strike next and who authorities and journalists thought he was. He now really *was* like the Hulk or Superman. People wanted to read theories about his strength, if he had a girlfriend or wife, and his possible secret identity.

Though the newsletter gave none of these answers, it gave the illusion that it would . . . if you just kept reading. It also gave people something exciting to talk about. Nnamdi included. He wanted to talk about risks, consequences, hero-ism, and battle plans. And he only wanted to talk about it all with Chioma. She always had the best ideas and knew how to put things into perspective, even when it was something he didn't necessarily want to hear. But she hadn't spoken to him in over two weeks, so he hadn't set things straight with her. *But she hasn't set things straight with me, either,* he thought. All day in school, he brooded. None of his friends would talk to him. And Chioma, though always nearby, still wouldn't look at him.

As he walked home, he was so deep in his thoughts that he nearly missed the green Hummer parked along the road. He stood there staring at its shiny golden grille. Then Nnamdi saw the man standing on the side of the road next to it. The Chief of Chiefs, again. Mere feet away. His back was to Nnamdi, his front to a television camera. To the left, a small crowd was gathering to listen and watch. Someone grabbed Nnamdi's shoulder and pulled him aside.

"Sorry, kid," a plump sweaty man in a tight suit said. He dabbed his brow with a handkerchief. "You were about to walk right into the camera's view."

"Sorry," Nnamdi muttered, turning back to stare at the Chief of Chiefs. This time, he felt no fear at the sight of him. No anxiety. Only outrage. Why was this man being put on TV? He was a criminal! A murderer!

"I'm just a humble businessman," the Chief was saying in his professor-like voice to the woman interviewing him. "A lot of people can't deal with a man who is successful legally. So they attach crazy stories to him. Really, I am no criminal."

"So you have no fear of the Man coming after you the way he did with Mama Go-Slow?"

Nnamdi's ears perked up.

"I fear the Man as any Kaleria citizen would," the Chief said. "We all saw what he did to an old woman. Obviously, he will attack anyone. Not just criminals."

Nnamdi felt the Man ripple beneath his skin, so he smiled to himself, despite his anger. He could just imagine the chaos if he changed into the Man and descended on the Chief of Chiefs like a shadow of revenge and it was all captured on camera. But then he thought of his father. Physically attacking the Chief of Chiefs for no clear reason was probably not how the Ikenga was meant to be used.

Nnamdi shoved his hands in his pockets and walked home. He needed a plan.

Nevertheless, that night, he didn't think when he sneaked out of the house and ran to Chioma's window. If he had, he'd never have chanced it. He'd been thinking all day and it was giving him nothing but a headache.

He threw a tiny pebble at Chioma's bedroom window on the second floor of the apartment building. He'd done this twice in the past. The first was two years ago, just before going to bed, when he'd caught one of those colorful grasshoppers she loved so much. And the second was months before his father was killed, when he heard that Chioma's grandmother had died and Chioma wouldn't come out of the house.

Finally, Chioma cracked open her window and she peeked out. She gazed at him for a moment and then shut the window. Nnamdi's shoulders slumped. Not even a hello. He was about to walk away when she came out of the front door, a jacket over her nightgown and flip-flops on her feet. Her braids were gathered together in a wrapped scarf.

She leaned against the wall with her arms over her chest. Nnamdi did the same. For minutes they said nothing. Feeling uncomfortable, Nnamdi looked at a spider creeping up the concrete wall of the apartment building. Chioma pushed around a piece of trash on the ground with the tip of her flip-flop. From one of the apartments, a baby cried. Nnamdi turned to Chioma, took a deep breath, and said, "I'm sorry."

She looked up, grinned, and threw her arms around him. "This time, you mean it," she said into his ear. Nnamdi tensed up. But then he relaxed. She smelled like the cinnamon she loved to pour into her oatmeal every morning.

"Here," he said, handing her the string of colorful beads he'd bought at the market after school. "In case you forget that I apologized sincerely."

She laughed, taking the beads. Nnamdi knew she liked anything with colors and a strong smell. He grinned when she sniffed them. He'd sprayed them with his mother's perfume. They sat on the concrete steps as she tied them around her wrist.

"A lot has been happening to me," he said as she put her bracelet on. He hesitated, biting his lip.

Chioma glanced at him and motioned for him to keep talking.

"Since that night I ran after that man during my father's memorial. You remember that?"

"Of course," she said. "I was the one who told you not to go out there."

"Chioma, I'm going to tell you something that will sound crazy. Just let me tell it all, then you talk, okay?"

She squinted at him. "Okay, but tell it fast. We both

have to get back home or we'll be in trouble."

Nnamdi looked at his shoes and blew out a breath. Then he looked at Chioma. There was no other way to say it. "I am the Man," he blurted.

Chioma frowned deeply. "What? You can't b—"

He held up a hand to stop her from talking; when she did, he quickly added, "*And* I think it's what made me almost hit you." He told her everything, from beginning to end. From his father's ghost giving him the Ikenga to the thrashing that Mama Go-Slow gave him. He told her about the anger that would sometimes overtake him and what it felt like to be a tall, super-strong shadow man. The more he spoke, the lighter he felt. And when he finished, he took a deep breath, looked at his hands, and smiled. Then he looked at Chioma's face and the smile dropped from his lips.

"Oh, Nnamdi," she sadly whispered.

"It's all right," he said. "I can't fully control it, but I can control it some, and see, I'm still alive."

She stood up. "I knew your father's death was hard on you, but I didn't know it was this bad."

"What?"

"Nnamdi, making up fantasies to work through your problems will not bring him back," she slowly said.

Nnamdi stood up. "Chioma, I didn't make any of that up! I'm not that good a liar or a storyteller."

"You're just missing your father," she insisted. "It's normal."

Nnamdi felt his temper flare burning hot and he stepped up to her, clenching his fists. "I'm TELLING the truth!" he harshly whispered.

However, this time, Chioma didn't get scared or cry. She waved a dismissive hand at him and made to go inside.

Instead of increased rage and violence, Nnamdi felt his temper instantly fizzle out. He looked at her questioningly, but her back was to him as she went inside.

"Get it together, man," she said over her shoulder. "I'll see you tomorrow. Thanks for the bracelet."

11

Senseless

"TO KILL THE snake, you cut off its head." That's what Nnamdi's mother had said. For Kaleria, the Chief of Chiefs was the snake's head. After being the Man for four weeks, Nnamdi finally felt he truly understood the root of the proverb. He had taken down two of Kaleria's worst criminals and beaten one into hiding (for Three Days' Journey hadn't been seen since Nnamdi had beaten him up that first night as the Man), but they were not the root of Kaleria's corruption problem. The Chief of Chiefs was that root. With the Chief of Chiefs still in power, Kaleria's crime ring would stay strong no matter what he did. Many nights after talking to Chioma, Nnamdi was lying in bed, rolling these thoughts around in his head, when he heard a voice.

"Please! This is my greatest possession!" the voice angrily pleaded. A man's voice. And he was sobbing. Nnamdi sat bolt upright, straining to hear the voice again. He turned to his bedroom window when he heard the gentle sobbing. He could even sense the direction from which it was coming as well as the distance. Nnamdi jumped out of bed. The path outside his window that ran past the garden was empty. The voice was in his head. Someone was in trouble; the Man had a task. He looked at his X-Men pencil case, inside which was the Ikenga, quiet and potent with strange power.

"Okay," Nnamdi whispered excitedly to himself. "I can do this!"

He slipped on his gym shoes, jeans, and a T-shirt, being careful not to make too much noise. His mother was a heavy sleeper, but if he banged on anything, she'd come and check on him. He opened his window and gently slipped out. Then he opened the gate a crack and took off down the road. As he ran, he could feel his pulse quicken and deepen. He gave in to it. Then he willed it. He felt his footsteps grow heavier, his legs longer. He ran faster. Judging from the intensity of the pleading, he had to hurry.

He ran for over a mile and there, on the dark and deserted road, he saw them. A white shiny BMW had stopped in the middle of the road and three men stood in front of the head-lights. Two of the men wore expensive suits. The other man wore shabby rags and Nnamdi could smell him from where he stood—a mixture of feces, sweat, and hair oil. The man in the rags, who was gently swaying, held the two well-dressed men at gunpoint.

For a moment, Nnamdi just stood there, feeling unsteady as his mind processed it all. This was Never Die, the man who had robbed his mother weeks ago. Nnamdi balled his fists.

"You be idiot?" Never Die growled. "You no see dis gun? GIVE ME DE KEYS!"

One of the men had the keys. They jiggled in his shaky hand. "This c-c-c-car, na my graduation presen—"

"Give me de keys here, abi you wan mek I blow your head?!" Never Die screamed. If this had been Three Days' Journey, the car thief, he'd never have allowed the men to exit the car with the keys. He'd have shoved the men out and made off with the car in a matter of seconds. Never Die wasn't as crafty.

Nnamdi was a shadow in the street and none of the men noticed him until he was practically on top of Never Die. The two men scrambled back as Nnamdi wrenched the gun from Never Die's hand and threw it aside. Never Die was squirmy and he managed to get free of Nnamdi's grasp for a moment. He pulled a switchblade from his tattered pocket and held it in front of him.

"The Man!" Never Die shrieked, looking him up and down with wild eyes.

Nnamdi's mind was on autopilot. He would subdue Never Die and make sure he was jailed, as Never Die should have been when he robbed and humiliated his mother weeks ago. He ran at Never Die and Never Die ran at him.

Never Die was a strong man and Nnamdi found himself starting to panic as the two grasped at each other's shoulders and arms. Nnamdi landed a punch, but Never Die came right back at him. There was a moment where Nnamdi had Never Die's arms, but then he twisted and got loose. *Oh no!* Nnamdi thought just before Never Die slashed him across the chest with his switchblade.

The pain was sharp and hot. Nnamdi roared and shoved Never Die back. He looked down at himself and only saw shadow, but he could feel wetness. Tears ran down his face. Mama Go-Slow had been brutal but she hadn't stabbed him. *Am I going to die?* he wondered. At the same time, crazed fury flooded his system. He bared his teeth, his rage fueled by the pain.

"Come on," Never Die taunted with a nervous laugh, taking a step back. "Give me reason to kill you."

Nnamdi slapped the knife from Never Die's hand and headbutted him. Never Die went down like a sack of yams. Then Nnamdi was on him, punching and slapping and kicking. Tears flew from his eyes as he beat Never Die. Memories of his humiliated and terrified mother fueled him, as did the hot sting of his stab wound. Nnamdi heard the sound of the car starting and screeching off. He'd saved the two men, but he didn't stop punching Never Die.

"Please!" Never Die wept. "Stop, o!"

Nnamdi didn't stop. He punched Never Die in the jaw. Then he punched him in the jaw again. He kicked him in the side. *Daddy was a failure*, Nnamdi thought, slapping Never Die one last time. *And now I am, too.* Never Die lay there, unmoving, his nose bleeding, his face swelling, his legs in a strange position. Nnamdi stood up, tall and shadowy. A hulking monster. But in his mind, he came back to himself, his thoughts clearing, the anger draining away. He blinked. He stared into the darkness, seeing the result of his actions clearly. Was Never Die dead? Had he killed him?

Nnamdi threw his head back. "YAAAAAAHHHHH!" he screamed. He turned and ran off.

12

Stuck

"OH MY GOD," Nnamdi whispered over and over as he made his way home. He still felt heavy and strong and his head was throbbing as if it were full of exploding stones. The night air was hot, pressing at his head. He was sweating. Or was that blood he felt dribbling down his belly? *Did I kill him? I might have killed him,* he thought. He made his way home only because his feet took him in that direction. A scrawny dog trotted out of an alley, took one look at him, whimpered, and scurried away.

"What am I?" he whispered. He looked at his arms. They were wrapped in shadow. His hands were the size of dinner plates and strong enough to crush rocks to dust. He heard himself breathing heavily, his mouth open. He sounded like an elephant. He stopped and touched his chest. He felt mangled flesh there, and wetness, though he could not see blood due to his body's darkness. This was *nothing* like what he'd imagined being a superhero would be like. If he'd killed someone, he was no better than the Chief of Chiefs. He was worse. A monster.

On the other side of the street he saw the akara lady, sitting at her stall, frying fresh akara over a flame. If she was out, it couldn't be really late at night. She usually went in around eleven. Her pot was empty. She was frying up her last batch of akara. She looked up at him as he passed on the other side of the one-way street. He could hear her gasp and her heart rate quicken. The akara lady stared at him and lifted a tentative hand, either a greeting or signaling him to stop. He kept running.

He scrambled up and over the wall in the back of the house, easily scaling the sharp glass and barbed wire. As he approached his window he slowed down. If Never Die was dead, he would never commit a crime again. So why wasn't Nnamdi changing back? By the time he got to his window, he was shuddering with panic. He could not let his mother see him like this. A violent monster. She'd think he'd come to rob or *kill* her. Regardless, at his size, he couldn't even fit through the window. He sat down in the grass in front of the window and leaned against the wall.

He might have killed a man tonight. He had not con-trolled his power. He hadn't just been angry. In the jumble of anger, outrage, and shock, he'd been consumed by rage. He could blame no one but himself for what he'd done. He crept to the garden. Maybe there he would calm down and shift back to himself. Maybe his father would even appear or at least speak to him. Maybe.

Nnamdi stood among his growing yams, tomatoes, onions, sunflower shoots, peppers, and herbs. The smell of this place would usually have soothed him. But in this state, his senses were heightened. The plants stank; the smells were too strong. The crickets and katydids sounded like sirens. There was a turkey in someone's pen that was not sleeping soundly; he could hear it restlessly ruffling its feathers. He could hear all the people in the apartment building and houses next door breathing deeply, sleeping in their beds; their lives were not complicated and messed up, like his. Someone turned over and farted. Someone snorted. Someone sighed. Then his entire body seized up, accompanied by waves of rage that flowed like fire in the veins of his hands. He gritted and ground his teeth, hissing and moaning at the pain.

He held his breath and counted to ten, hoping it would stop. Then he erupted, grasping handfuls of onion stalks and yanking, tearing at the delicate sunflower stems, stomping on the tomatoes, kicking, clawing, ripping. Lastly, he mashed and mashed the yams into mush. He stormed to the half-closed window of his bedroom and put his fist right through it. *CRASH!*

"What was that!" he heard his mother shout. "Nnamdi?! Are you all right?"

Nnamdi looked from side to side, holding his painful fist. But no matter where he looked, he couldn't focus, not with his eyes or his mind. His veins heated with burning rage again and he bit down on his tongue to stifle a scream. He tasted blood in his mouth as he heard his bedroom door opening. *Can't let her see me!* he thought, running to the gate, nearly knocking over a sleep-weary Mr. Oke. He shoved the gate open and it banged hard on the wall. Nnamdi loped off into the night.

13

Dark Time of the Soul

HE FLED TO the one place where he had always found peace: the abandoned school down the road. He came here when he needed quiet. Abandoned long before he was born, the school was a forgotten place and thus a good place to go to forget. Chioma had told him that a young wealthy couple had returned to Nigeria from America with hopes of making things better in Kaleria. Sadly, they were set upon by Mama Go-Slow, Never Die, Three Days' Journey, and several scammers. Within a year, the couple had abandoned their project and fled back to the United States, nearly broke.

The abandoned school had four thick concrete walls, a sturdy but unfinished roof, and several rooms. And all were covered with creeping vines. A nest of noisy weaverbirds sat in one of the corners. A lizard scurried across his foot. A few damaged desks had been left behind and plants had begun to grow into the glassless windows. Nnamdi looked at the wall near the back, where the phrase *He who is afraid of doing too much always does too little* was engraved into the cement in ornate writing. This sentence usually inspired him, but tonight it didn't. The small flowerpot on the windowsill where Chioma had planted a mystery seed was still there and he resisted the urge to smash it.

Nnamdi groaned, staring up at the concrete ceiling and the night sky through the holes where it had collapsed. His belly was empty, his mind was clouded, his fists were clenched with fury, and his heart was heavy. He curled up in his corner, right there on the floor. In the darkness, he heard night creatures scurrying about. He felt mosquitoes trying to penetrate his skin and probably lapping up his leaking blood. He shivered, remembering the thick, meaty sound of his fist connecting with Never Die's face. He whimpered and then his body clenched up with a hot wave of rage. *What if I killed him?* Nnamdi thought, closing his eyes. *Isn't how I thought it would be. I'm no hero.*

Poor Nnamdi fell into a restless sleep.

Birds tweeted. Nnamdi opened his eyes to the leafy ceiling of the abandoned school. Outside, the bright sun shone. He looked at his hands. He looked at his body. He was still the Man. He was stuck. He pounded a fist on a desk and it cracked into three pieces.

He deserved this.

Nnamdi was a shadow. He stood over seven feet tall with superhuman strength, but he was nobody. His clothes, which disappeared when he was the Man and reappeared when he changed back, seemed to have disappeared for good. He could feel the wind directly on his skin. When he stepped into sunlight, it seemed to reject him; the sunlight would not touch his shadowy body. And then there was the rage pulsing through him like radioactive poison injected into his veins. It made it hard for him to think.

By the third day, Nnamdi had punched through one of the school walls with his fists, uprooted three large trees, and smashed all but one of the desks into pieces. He was dangerous and he knew it, so he only left the abandoned school when he couldn't take the hunger any longer. When the sun set, he went begging, seeking out sellers who had stalls in the darkness.

There was only one seller who did not run away from him. She sold groundnuts and only frowned at his gruff, angry voice and hunched shadowy figure. "I've seen stranger things than you," she told him. She gave him some of her leftovers and some of her remaining bags of "pure water" when it was late at night. He would quickly thank her and be off before she could muster up the nerve to ask him any questions. He'd eat the groundnuts in a few gulps, barely chewing, not tasting the food at all.

Was his mother looking for him? Did the newsletter run

stories about him and how he was one of Kaleria's latest missing children? Or even worse, did it run stories about how
the Man had murdered somebody? He did not know what
day it was. He barely remembered what it felt like to be the
twelve-year-old boy that he had been. He'd lost his way and
he wasn't interested in finding it. The boy named Nnamdi
retreated to a corner in his mind, where he curled up and let
the darkness envelop him like the waters of a disastrous flood.

"Nnamdi?" Chioma's voice echoed far into the room he'd
locked himself in, where he was curled up in a sea of darkness. Her voice touched his ears.

His world stood still.

Nnamdi, he thought. *That's my name.* She was at the
far end of the large schoolroom in the doorless doorway. She
stepped one of her sandaled feet onto the concrete, keeping
the other in the overgrown grass. The sun shone in behind
her, making her nothing but a shadow. "Nnamdi," she said
again. "Is that you?"

He slowly stood up, grasping a piece of the freshly
buckled concrete. He shook his head, trying to clear and
focus his mind. Instead, his temples throbbed and this made
him even angrier. He pounded a fist against his leg. Across the
large room, Chioma cautiously crept through the door, tightly
grasping her backpack. Her braids were down and she pushed
one from her face, her eyes settling on Nnamdi. She saw him;
she shuddered and took a step back.

"Go away!" Nnamdi shouted, his voice deep and pow-erful. The lizards in the building skittered in various direc-tions, all away from him. Some ran out the windows, some out the doorway, some scurried around Chioma's feet. They sounded like scraping paper. The walls were suddenly alive with the quick movement of hundreds of orange and green and brown lizards.

"I *knew* it was you!" she shouted back, her voice shaky with emotion. "I've been thinking and thinking about it. . . . You did it, didn't you? How could you?!" she screamed, her voice cracking. "You're . . . you're just as bad as the man who killed your father!"

She whimpered as Nnamdi growled deep in his throat.

"What's happened to you?" she whispered. "What . . ."

Using all his strength, he threw the concrete. When it left his hand, he grunted with satisfaction. Any violence he produced decreased the burning in his body. The sharp, jag-ged piece of concrete buried itself deep in the wall behind Chioma.

She screeched, turned, about to run out the door. But something made her stop. She relaxed her shoulders and turned back around.

Nnamdi threw another chunk. "I HATE YOU!"

He threw another and another. Chioma didn't move as she glared bravely at Nnamdi. He was tired; he was spent. There was a hole beside him now where he'd dug up the concrete. He examined her face more closely. She looked determined, her nostrils flared, her eyebrows creased, her lips pressed together. He could hear her rapid heartbeat. She was terrified. She was grasping her backpack's straps. Her eyes were dry. His friend since they had been babies. Chioma had always been there.

Nnamdi shut his eyes, crouched to the ground, and curled his body as tightly as possible. He needed to protect himself; he needed to protect Chioma. Moments passed and everything was quiet. She had left. Good. He retreated further into himself.

Nnamdi felt someone take his hand. Chioma's hand was tiny on top of his, but it was also firm and warm. She grasped his hand as if she would not let go. He was nearly twice her height, four times her weight, and he was sure she could not *see* his face. And unlike Mama Go-Slow, Chioma knew nothing about juju. Yet still, somehow Chioma *saw* Nnamdi.

"You can't hurt me," she whispered close to his ear. Then she leaned forward and threw her arms around him. Nnamdi certainly was not small, but now he *felt* as if he were.

Behind his eyes, Nnamdi let himself remember what seemed like a time light-years away. Two years ago he and Chioma had sat outside in his father's garden on the hottest day of the year, playing tic-tac-toe on Chioma's phone. It was a Saturday night, and rather than waste fuel running air-conditioning, everyone in the neighborhood had decided to go outside, even the younger children. It was all rather magical.

Nnamdi had been in the garden, reading an *X-Men* comic book by flashlight, when Chioma had come walking by on her way to her cousin's house. When Chioma saw him, she decided to join him instead, sending her cousin a quick text. They'd laughed and laughed over the game, enjoying how evenly matched they were. Neither of them had a care in the world that evening, the stars twinkled above in the clear sky, and the garden's night flowers made the air smell so sweet. Back then Nnamdi had no reason to be so serious or angry. No one was wondering where either of them were. Light-years away.

"Everyone thinks the Man kidnapped you. They're even talking about him possibly killing your father," Chioma whispered, still hugging him. "It's ridiculous."

Nnamdi's body was still prickled with heat, his mind still clouded, though less than it had been when she'd first arrived. "You were a really big story in the newsletter," she continued. "Your mother said the window to your bedroom had been smashed and there was blood on it. So horrible! You mashed up the garden, too. Even your yams. The police interviewed your mother, me, your friends at school. None of us knew anything. I didn't tell about all you told me because I didn't think it would help. I didn't really believe it . . . not yet. Took me a day or so. Plus, I knew it would all just end up in the newsletter." She paused, pulling her arms away. He heard her shift to sit beside him.

"After a few days, we heard nothing. It didn't make sense. The Man wasn't a killer or kidnapper," she said.

"The Man *is* a killer," Nnamdi growled.

"No," Chioma said. She paused. "Nnamdi, I started thinking about everything and . . . Well, I came here."

Chioma continued talking and Nnamdi listened. She told him that Never Die was alive. He was in Kaleria's hospital receiving the best treatment money could buy. The town was treating him like a victim instead of a criminal. He told authorities that he'd been thinking of robbing two men but then the Man had attacked him and beaten him nearly to death. All Nnamdi focused on were the basics: *Never Die is alive*, he thought. *I didn't kill him.* He opened his mouth and breathed in the truth.

He burst into tears. *I'm not a* monster, he thought. *I'm Nnamdi Icheteka and I was trying to do the right thing! Everything just got out of control . . . somehow.* Chioma held him tightly as he wept. And gently, he laid his head on Chioma's shoulder and, bit by bit, he felt the anger drain from him like air from a deflating balloon. As his anger retreated, his body shrunk, and the darkness of the Man went away. He changed back to himself. His clothes were filthy and nearly rags.

"When . . . whenever you change into the Man, the shadows around me stretch," she said. "I didn't understand before, but I understand it all now. It is just like that day I caught the big blue butterfly in the garden three years ago, when your father's shadow was so long and mighty. When you change, normal shadows around me look like the super-long shadows you see in the late evening. It doesn't matter if it's morning or afternoon! You never want to know what shadows look like at night. It's scary." More tears poured from her eyes. "Maybe you do know." She gazed at him for several moments. "Nnamdi, since you've been missing, I've been living in constant shadows."

"It must be because you touched the Ikenga," Nnamdi said weakly.

"Ikenga?" she asked.

Nnamdi sat up and, for the second time, told Chioma everything. This time she really listened. He would never forget the fascinated look on her face.

Tap tap tap.

Chioma handed Nnamdi her backpack, where she'd stuffed a change of clothes she'd gotten from her father's room. "I had a feeling you'd need these. The pants are going to be huge but . . ."

"They'll be fine," Nnamdi said. "Thanks."

"I brought some snacks, too. Some chin chin, groundnuts, and some plantain chips."

"Okay," Nnamdi said, looking into the bag of groundnuts. "But why so much?"

"Because we're not going home yet," she said. She spoke fast. "Now that I've found you here, I know it was all really real and if we don't do this thing, Kaleria will burn."

Nnamdi sighed, shoving a handful of groundnuts into his mouth. "What are you talking about?"

"You promise you won't think I'm crazy?" she asked.

Nnamdi cocked his head and popped more groundnuts into his mouth as he stared hard at Chioma until she laughed. "Fair enough," she said.

"Just talk," he said. "We've moved beyond crazy."

"Well, a few days ago, I was coming home from my cous- in's house. It was late evening and the sun was going down, so I was hurrying. I came to the intersection near your house."

Nnamdi held his breath. Was it *the* intersection? The one where his father's ghost had appeared and given him the Ikenga?

"I noticed a man under a streetlight," she continued. "He was looking at me. I'd have kept going if . . . if he hadn't looked familiar somehow. The way he stood, his green beret, the way he *looked*. I thought maybe my eyes were tricking me or it was the weird light of dusk. Sometimes things can look strange. He motioned that I should come to him. I don't know why I did. When I got close, it was scary, because I still couldn't quite see his face, no matter how hard I looked.

It was like my eyes wouldn't focus. And things got swimmy, or something. It was hard for me to focus on anything." She paused, searching Nnamdi's face.

"Go on," he said. "Did he say anything?"

"Does this sound—"

"It sounds no weirder than what I've been going through, Chioma. What'd he say?"

"I think it was your father," she blurted.

"I know."

"How's that possible?"

"How's any of this possible, Chioma?"

"You really think it's because I touched that Ikenga? Ikengas are just supposed to protect houses and stuff."

"What did he say, Chioma?" Nnamdi insisted.

"He said if you weren't going to listen, he would tell me. He said it's quiet and slow for now, but Kaleria is heading toward *flames*."

Nnamdi felt a deep icy sensation in the pit of his belly. He'd had the very same dream on the first night he'd changed into the Man. "Did . . . did he say anything about stopping it?" Nnamdi asked.

She nodded. "We have to find a car that's been stolen. That will lead us toward the problem."

"But not *solve* it," Nnamdi said.

"Yeah. It felt like a riddle," she said. "All these random hints and details, and it was up to me to figure it out."

"Why can't he just be straightforward?" Nnamdi said. "If we need to do something, just say what we need to do."

"Because maybe we can't do it unless we truly understand what we're doing," Chioma said. "It's not about the answers to a riddle; it's about what you learn by solving it."

"Whatever," Nnamdi muttered.

"I know which car," Chioma said. "Your mother's friend Bonny's car was stolen two days ago."

"Had to be Three Days' Journey," he said, understanding now that Chioma was several steps ahead of him. "Ah, so we're going to Tse-Kucha."

She nodded.

Nnamdi chuckled. "Bonny's probably dying of sadness. He loves that car like his child."

14

The Riskiest, Stupidest, Most Irrational Thing

NNAMDI COULD NOT believe what he was doing. This was the riskiest, stupidest, most irrational thing he'd ever done. "My mother is going to go mad," Chioma said. Nnamdi wanted to disagree with Chioma. He wanted to tell her that her mother would understand when all was said and done, but he knew that would be a complete lie. They sneaked to the garden, where Chioma said she'd buried some rainy-day money, right at the base of the mango tree. Then Nnamdi had sneaked into his bedroom through his window and gotten some clothes and his savings, which wasn't much because he'd recently spent most of it on comic books. Surprisingly, his mother was not home. He'd paused, standing in the middle of his room. It had only been a few days, but so much had happened that it felt like years since he'd been in here.

They had just enough for the bus tickets and some extra snacks for later. The bus driver had looked at them strangely when they asked to buy tickets. But as soon as they showed him the money, he turned a blind eye to how young they were. Now Nnamdi and Chioma were sitting on a bus speeding down the highway. Nnamdi was already missing and now, when Chioma did not come home, she would be declared missing, too. Her parents were going to be so worried. But they decided it was best not to leave a note because in it they'd either have to lie or be so vague that everyone would only worry more.

"We'll find Bonny's car and then come home as soon as we can," Nnamdi said again, even though they had already agreed to this before setting off on their journey.

He looked away. The same thing had to be on both of their minds and he didn't want her to ask it: *How are we going to get home?* They didn't have enough money. Would they have to call their parents? *We'll cross that bridge when we get to it*, he thought. There were more urgent matters at hand.

If it was Three Days' Journey who took the car, then it was definitely in Tse-Kucha. Nnamdi's father had been trying to destroy a car-theft ring there for years. Nnamdi's mother, however, had an interest in Tse-Kucha for a wholly different reason. When Nnamdi's father was alive, Nnamdi's mother used to drive there and return with all kinds of delicious mangoes, her favorite food. Then his mother would invite her friends and have a mango-eating party. Chioma always came over and enjoyed eating mangoes with his mother and her friends more than Nnamdi did.

Tse-Kucha was over five hours away due to bad roads and go-slow. According to his father, it always took Three Days' Journey three days because he liked to drive the stolen cars slowly and make many stops to visit his many wives along the way. Three Days' Journey had a wife in every tiny village that lay between Kaleria and Tse-Kucha.

Nnamdi tried to nap on the bus, but a baby in the seat behind them kept screeching and carrying on. He was exhausted. He hadn't even had a chance to bathe since they'd left the abandoned school. He'd grabbed fresh clothes when he'd sneaked into his room for his savings, but clean clothes did not mean a clean body.

Beside him, Chioma, always the heavy sleeper, dozed. Nnamdi looked out the window as he ate some of the crispy akara. What would they do when they got to Tse-Kucha? He shut his eyes. He was the Man. When he'd caught Bad Market, he'd found him by stopping and concentrating. Could he find a car in the same way? he wondered.

After three hours, the late-afternoon sun was heavy in the sky as it prepared to set. Nnamdi had been to Tse-Kucha once with his mother and her friends about two years ago and he'd really enjoyed that trip. Because his mother had been with her friends, he was mostly left alone to observe and think. The town had been small and smelled sweet from all the mangoes. And he had to admit, the fruits were delicious. There were small homes and even a few huts. An active market. He couldn't recall any car garages or many cars at all, now that he thought of it. But there was a computer repair shop near the market. He remembered that because when they'd passed it, it had been full of people.

He focused his mind on the shop because it might be a good place to ask questions. The dirt road ran in front of it. The sign, what had the sign said? Surprised, he grinned as he recalled it perfectly: SUNSHINE COMPUTING. There was a stand in front of it beside boxes of mangoes. He saw that sign, too. It said, FREE MANGO WITH ANY REPAIR!!

"Cool," Nnamdi whispered, his eyes closed. This wasn't a memory anymore. This had to be another of the Man's abilities.

There was a small line there right now. Nnamdi could see it. Three women and ten men. Some carried cell phones, one carried a cube-shaped computer, and several carried laptops. All of them looked impatient and irritated. A young man was walking up the line, offering them each a mango while they waited.

"No, thank you. I have more than enough at home," snapped a woman carrying a cell phone. "This man needs to hurry up."

Cars passed on the road, sending up plumes of dust. Now

Nnamdi's powerful mind's eye could see inside the shop as two young men sat at a large table, parts and pieces all around them, peering into an open computer. They spoke quietly between themselves as they worked. Behind them, a woman wearing jeans and a T-shirt and carrying what looked like CDs or DVDs was exiting the back door. Nnamdi decided to follow her.

The woman walked onto a path that led between two walls of trees, humming to herself as she went. The path soon opened to a field full of cars. Some were dusty and some were sparkling clean. A few boys were scrubbing one of the dusty ones using a bucket of soapy water. They anxiously glanced at the woman and then worked faster. Then Nnamdi saw it: Bonny's prized blue Mercedes. It was near the back of the lot, to the right. It sparkled and shone in the sunlight. Out of all the cars, it looked the nicest. A few feet away, standing beside an old yellow Jeep, was Three Days' Journey. He was talking to the woman now, putting his arm around her. She took his arm away and stepped back, rolling her eyes.

Nnamdi pulled his mind back, trying to get the lay of the land in relation to Bonny's car. Doing so must have overworked his ability, because nausea washed over him and his forehead throbbed. Barely, he held on to the vision. Tse-Kucha. It was a small town. "Got it," he whispered, swallowing the saliva in his mouth. He opened his eyes to find Chioma looking at him. "Chioma," he said breathlessly. "Do you have any of that minty gum you always carry? Please say you do. I don't feel well."

She quickly rummaged around in her backpack and brought out a piece. Nnamdi could have kissed her. "Oh, THANK you," he said, snatching it from her, removing the wrapper, and shoving it into his mouth. The last thing he needed was to vomit on the bus. The driver would probably kick them off. The minty flavor burst into his mouth like crisp, cool water, cleansing, calming. He sighed, feeling much better, though his forehead still pounded.

"What was that about?" Chioma asked.

"I don't know," he said. "A side effect? I was . . . I was seeing," he said. "I think that's what made me nauseous."

"You were going to throw up? Ew."

Nnamdi rolled his eyes.

Chioma laughed. "Are you all right now?"

"I think so. Just a headache. Chioma, I know where we have to go when we get there."

"Good, because I think I figured out something else. You know Ruff Diamond? He's been kidnapped and he's probably in Tse-Kucha, too."

"What?! How do . . ."

"Shh," she said, looking around. "When we stop for the next bathroom break."

Nnamdi had to wait two agonizing hours. The bus was hot and stuffy. A couple near the front of the bus got into a terrible argument that left the woman crying and the man moving to another seat. The baby behind them shrieked for an hour straight until she finally burped and went to sleep. And a man a few seats in front talked loudly on his cell phone the entire two hours and was still talking when they stopped and the driver proclaimed that everyone should "Get off for a few minutes and piss if you want to piss, or eat something if you dey hungry! We've got two more hours' drive."

They'd stopped on the side of the road next to a small market. The driver must have had some sort of deal with the people here. They sold all kinds of snacks and drinks and seemed to have been waiting for the bus. They charged twenty naira to use the restroom, a small zinc shack that stank like a burning zoo. The man who had been blabbing on his phone all through the bus trip was the first to pay to use the restroom. He brought out his phone as soon as he was finished and continued his conversation. Chioma tried unsuccessfully to bargain with the bathroom man and they ended up spending a sixth of their money to use the facilities. Afterward, Nnamdi and Chioma could only afford skewers of *suya* and shared a bottle of water. They walked a few steps away from the other passengers and stood beside a tall tree.

"You never know who's on the bus and might be listening," Chioma said.

Nnamdi nodded. He quickly told her about his new ability and all he'd seen.

"That's really . . . Wow!" she said. "So you know exactly where his car is?"

Nnamdi grinned and nodded.

"You're a walking GPS!"

"I guess. Except using it too much makes me want to vomit," he said. "But, Chioma, what's this about Ruff Diamond? Hurry, tell me everything."

"Remember when Ruff Diamond left school?"

"Yeah," he said. It was days before Nnamdi had fought with Never Die. "Jide said he heard Ruff Diamond went to see his mother."

"We leave in two minutes!" the bus driver announced.

Chioma and Nnamdi talked faster. "You'd been gone for a few days," Chioma said. "You know . . . you were at the abandoned school. Well, Ruff Diamond went to visit his mother and he hasn't come back."

"So?" Nnamdi said, shrugging. "That doesn't mean he's been kidnapped."

"I know that. I'm not finished," Chioma said. She took a quick swig of water. "You know how my laptop broke and my father won't buy me a new one until next year? Well, I wanted to write some poems and I offered Ruff Diamond some cookies I made in exchange for using his laptop for a few days, so he lent it to me. This was the day before he supposedly went to his mother's house. Well, he never came back for it or called me or anything. His laptop is really nice and he worked for his uncle for a year and a half before his uncle would buy it for him. That's not something you leave behind. Now it's been over a week!"

"Everyone!" the bus driver shouted. "We are leaving!"

They started walking back to the bus. "Anyway, I was in the market, buying tomatoes for my mum from Ruff Diamond's auntie, when his uncle came running to her. They moved away from me and were whispering. His auntie started weeping. I tried to listen. All I caught was 'What kind of ransom?' His uncle was holding a mango. One of those nice fat sweet ones. And he threw it on the ground. I didn't think anything of it before, other than 'What a waste!' But now . . ."

"All the pieces fit," Nnamdi said, finishing her thought. "You can't get those big, big mangoes from anywhere nearby except in Tse-Kucha."

Chioma nodded.

They were standing outside the full bus.

"And if it involves Tse-Kucha . . . I'll bet Three Days' Journey had something to do with it," Nnamdi said.

"Yeah," Chioma agreed.

"Are you two getting on or what?" the driver asked, poking his head out the door. They scrambled back onto the bus and the driver quickly shut the door behind them and started the engine.

15

Tse-Kucha

NNAMDI RECOGNIZED EVERYTHING from his vision as soon as they got off the bus. "It's just down that road," he said.

"What is? The computer place?"

"Yeah."

"Ah!" Chioma exclaimed, slapping her arm. "Mosquitoes here do not wait one moment."

Nnamdi slapped the side of his head. When his hand came away, there were two crushed mosquitoes on it. More would come out in the dark, but he was glad the sun was setting. These days, the darkness was his friend.

They stood behind the tree right outside the shop. It hadn't taken them more than a half hour to get to the place from the bus stop. There was no line anymore, but the lights inside were on and the two computer technicians inside were hard at work. Since it was dusk, Nnamdi wouldn't have any trouble sneaking up to the entrance unnoticed.

"The car isn't far from here," Nnamdi said. "I'm going to . . . change. Then I'll go in and get a feel for the place. Maybe I can learn where the keys are. Follow me to the door, but stay out here and listen in."

Chioma nodded. "I'll whistle if I see someone coming." She grinned. "Go on. Change. I want to see this!"

"Right," he said. He exhaled, relaxed, and focused on their task of retrieving Bonny's precious car. Then he shifted into the Man. The change came easily and that gave him a bit of confidence. However, he was still scared.

"Woooooow," Chioma said.

"Be careful, okay?" he said, trying to stay focused. "Don't try anything crazy."

"I should be telling *you* that," she said. She took his big hand. "Don't . . . don't *kill* anyone."

"I won't," he said firmly.

"And don't get killed either."

They scrambled across the empty street and Nnamdi went inside. A bell on the door rang as he entered.

"*Weu! Weu! Weu!* It is an evil spirit! Don't hurt us, o!" one of the young men cried when he saw the Man coming. He looked about twenty years old, was muscular like a wrestler, and was as tall as Nnamdi's father, yet he was shrieking and cowering against the wall. Nnamdi was disgusted.

"We have money, o!" the other said. He looked older than his partner, yet he had tears in his eyes and was breathing like he was about to die. "In . . . in the back, we . . ."

"Shut up!" Nnamdi roared. "There are cars in a lot not far from here. I know this place is involved. Where are the car keys?"

The two men froze.

"If neither of you speaks, both of you will be hurt." He grabbed the one who was not crying and lifted him up.

"The keys aren't here! There's a woman! She is the boss. Her name's Mrs. Puneneh! She carries the keys with her. She's on her way here! Just . . ."

There was a click from the back of the room and the back door swung open. A tall man in dirty jeans and an even dirt-ier T-shirt walked in carrying a bag of garbage. He swayed a bit, obviously a little drunk. Nnamdi had seen this man before and he knew precisely how to deal with him. He turned to Chioma at the front door. "Chioma, go find her! She's tall and kind of mean looking!"

"But—"

"Go, Chioma! Go find that lady before she gets away!"

She ran off. Nnamdi sighed, relieved. He didn't want her to see what he was about to do.

"Three Days' Journey," Nnamdi bellowed, turning to the swaying drunken man.

Three Days' Journey dropped the garbage. "What the

hell?! You again?!" He reached into his pocket. Nnamdi felt his heart somersault. He leapt to the side just as Three Days' Journey brought the gun out and fired. *BLAM!* A computer monitor caved in where Nnamdi had been moments before. Nnamdi moved like the wind, his mind calming so completely that it nearly shut down. He was in the zone, sure of where he needed to move and how he needed to do it. His life depended on all this.

"Oof!" Three Days' Journey gasped as Nnamdi threw his body into him. They went crashing to the floor beside a wall. Nnamdi grabbed Three Days' Journey by the arm and he tried to twist and squirm himself free. With his other hand, Nnamdi grabbed the gun.

"Ayeee!" Three Days' Journey shrieked. "Leave me! Leave me! Ahhhhh!" He shoved a dirty bare foot into Nnamdi's gut. The man stank worse than putrid garbage.

Something smashed against the back of Nnamdi's head and he dropped the gun.

"Ha!" one of the men shouted. "Take that!" The laptop crashed to the ground behind Nnamdi and he could feel bits of plastic hit the backs of his legs.

Nnamdi shuddered, fire in his veins. He saw the edges of the world go reddish black. He could crush stone with his bare hands. He could kill all three of these men. His head ached from the blow. Three Days' Journey was kicking him in the belly and each kick felt like death. He'd managed to stay on his feet all this time, but he knew he would fall soon. Where was the gun?

Nnamdi tried to turn from Three Days' Journey to look for it and that's when the other man jumped on his back and began to strangle him with his hands.

"Yes! That's it!" Three Days' Journey screeched. "*This* is the idiot who has been messing up our business in Kaleria. Take him down! Stop him! There is a large reward! Then we can get on with our business!"

A thousand things went through Nnamdi's mind and each moment brought more pain. But then he saw it in his mind. The dream of his home, his town, the place that his father had worked so hard to protect, the place his father died for, on fire. The death of his father all for nothing.

He flung the man from his back; he got up and ran off. Nnamdi whirled around and grabbed Three Days' Journey. His mind was in the red-and-black haze as he slammed Three Days' Journey against the wall again and again. Finally, Three Days' Journey went limp.

"Nnamdi!"

He dropped Three Days' Journey and whipped around. There Chioma was, standing behind the door, her eyes wide as she stared at him. He opened the door while keeping an eye on the remaining man who now cowered against the wall.

"Snap out of it!" she said. "Before you *kill* someone!"

Nnamdi shook his head and his mind cleared. "I . . ." He

looked at the unconscious Three Days' Journey.

"He's okay, I think," Chioma said. "See? He just moved a bit. Come on," she said. "Before he fully wakes up!" She raised her hand and shook a large set of keys.

Then Nnamdi's eye fell on the coil of copper wiring. "One thing first," he said, reaching for it.

"I saw her coming to the shop just like that guy said she would," Chioma said as Nnamdi wrapped another coil of copper around Three Days' Journey's arms. "She heard all the fighting and thought it was the police!" Chioma laughed. "She was too scared to go in. So I said, 'Mrs. Puneneh, give me the keys; Three Days' Journey told me to get them.' She just wanted to get out of there."

"You should go away," Three Days' Journey spat, his nose bleeding all over the front of his filthy shirt. He pulled at his bound hands and grunted angrily. "What are you? Some sort of masquerade? Once I get out of these things, I'll send hell after you! This is MY business! My merchandise! My—"

Nnamdi shoved one of the black cloths the computer technicians used to clean dust from the computer screens into Three Days' Journey's mouth. "When your friends find you, you tell them the Man did this," he growled at the technician who was bound beside Three Days' Journey. He leaned closer to them. "You tell them that I am an evil spirit who does evil on people who *do* evil." The technician who was *not* crying looked horrified and then he, too, began to sniffle. Even Three Days' Journey stopped trying to shout through the cloth in his mouth.

"Oh my God," Chioma groaned. "What are you crying for? As if you're the one being maltreated. Thieves *and* cowards! You should all be ashamed."

"Forget them," Nnamdi said. "Let's go."

They exited the back door into the night.

"I know this place," he said. He'd seen it in his mind. They were close. He relaxed and shut his eyes. His mind was like a map. He opened his eyes. "That way!" he said. He looked toward the opening in the trees. "Take my hand," he said. He felt Chioma's small familiar hand in his large one. "There's a path."

The lot looked like it used to be for football before it housed at least fifty stolen cars. Nnamdi looked at the keys. They were each labeled with a number. The cars were, too. Thankfully, the pattern and arrangement was easy to figure out. At least they wouldn't have to try a whole bunch of keys to start Mr. Bonny's car. But finding which key wasn't the problem; the problem was that they didn't know how to drive.

"Nnamdi, wait," she said. "I didn't want to say it in there in front of those idiots, but after she threw the keys at me, she said, 'Tell him I'll see to the hostages!' "

"Tell who? Three Days' Journey? Hostage*s*?! It's not just Ruff Diamond?"

"Oh! So it's a whole scamming ring! My mom's been saying that's been happening a lot lately. They take people from rich families."

"Where are they being held?" Nnamdi asked.

"How should I know?! Try to locate them with your 'GPS power'!"

Nnamdi frowned and then he blinked, realizing what she meant. "Oh," Nnamdi said. "Yeah!" He leaned against one of the cars as another thought came to him. "Do you think that kidnapping people is what leads to Kaleria's downfall?"

Chioma shrugged. "Maybe, it's everything. Kidnapping, thieves, killing. Maybe corruption is like a fuel and all it needs is one spark to set it on fire."

Nnamdi nodded. "So not one bad thing but many . . . piling up."

"Yes, yes," Chioma said, impatient. "But one thing at a time, Nnamdi. Find Ruff Diamond. And hurry. Who knows how long before Three Days' Journey's guys come looking for us?"

"Okay . . . right . . . shhh," he said, gathering his senses. "Don't make a sound, okay?"

Chioma nodded. She leaned against a car and waited. Nnamdi knew she wanted to ask him a question, but instead she kept quiet. She was focused . . . as he had to be. He

shifted his attention to his other friend, Ruff Diamond. Ruff
Diamond liked to talk and look at girls. He liked mangoes, like
Chioma. Nnamdi latched on to that. And soon his mind's
eye was pulled away from the lot full . . . *of cars. That way.*
He could see it. A white house surrounded by a concrete gate.
But the gate was open. A new golden one was being installed.
Though it was nighttime, Nnamdi could see it all.

Through the open half-built, half-disassembled gate, past a
shiny black SUV and two dusty old cars in the large driveway.
To a window on the lower part of the three-story house. Down
and into a basement. Full of people. Sweating. Some sitting,
others standing. There! Ruff Diamond!

He was sitting in a corner, staring blankly at a wall. He
wore jeans and his favorite red shirt, but the armpits and belly
were dark with sweat. A tall woman was standing before him.
She was wearing fresh clothes and makeup. She brought her
hand back and slapped him across the face.

"That Puneneh woman is there already," Nnamdi said,
opening his eyes. "There are many hostages, not just Ruff
Diamond. Some who don't seem to have been there long." For
a moment, he had a hard time focusing and he leaned to the
side a little. Chioma moved closer, propping him up.

"Are you all right?"

Nnamdi nodded. "Head hurting again," he said. "Let's go."

But he felt nauseous, too. And more than out of sorts.
It was worse than before, on the bus. No time for him to

worry about that now, though. The Puneneh woman must have connected his presence with Ruff Diamond. Maybe she even thought Ruff Diamond's parents had called the police. Who knew what she was going to do to him now?

"Chioma, see that car on the far left? The blue Mercedes?"

Chioma looked for a long moment and then nodded.

"That's Bonny's car. Get it started," he said. His forehead was painfully pounding and he breathed through his mouth in order not to vomit. He groaned and then forced himself to stand up straight. "Turn on the lights when you see me come back. And if . . . if I don't come back . . ."

"You'll come back," she snapped. Her eyes glazed, but she didn't let her tears fall. She took the keys, focused.

"I don't know how we are going to get the car out, but . . ."

"I can drive," Chioma said.

"What?"

Chioma only shook her head. "I have idiot older cousins who thought it was funny to teach an eight-year-old. Nearly got me killed. But taught me a lot, too. It's a long story. Go get Ruff Diamond!"

Nnamdi ran through the bushes as fast as his powerful legs would take him. It was about a third of a mile between the parking lot and the house. He still felt ill but he pushed through it. Time was of the essence. His sharp eyes saw right through the darkness and he arrived at the open gate in no time. The white house with the half-gold and half-white gate loomed. From where he stood he could hear something happening in the basement. The footsteps of many people. Shouting. The sound of a gun firing. Screams. It was deep night now and Nnamdi was glad for the cover of darkness as he ran across the driveway. He heard more shots at the front door. He tried to open it, but it was locked.

Ruff Diamond's in there, he thought. *Maybe he's been shot.* This thought cleared his mind and chased away his nausea. He grasped the doorknob and, controlling his force, shoved the door open. The hinges cracked loudly. It swung open the rest of the way, revealing an empty hallway. No guards. *They must all be downstairs*, Nnamdi thought. He ran inside, following the screams and shouts.

The rest of what happened was a blank for Nnamdi; it was like a veil had been placed over his eyes when he wasn't looking and something beyond him was erasing his mind. When he finally came back to himself, he was still the Man, standing tall in the high-ceilinged basement. There were about twenty people standing around him staring. There was a puddle of vomit in the corner.

Mrs. Puneneh was lying on the floor, unconscious, in an awkward position, her nose bleeding. There was a crushed gun at his feet. Three angry, pummeled-looking men were tied to pipes with extension cords and being held down by eight sweaty men and women. And three more unconscious men were on the floor. Nnamdi's huge fists ached and there was a piercing pain in his left leg. He had a horrible taste in his mouth.

"Are you all right?" a woman asked.

Nnamdi only looked at her.

"At least he stopped vomiting," a man said.

"Is he even human?" another man asked. "Maybe bullets do not wound him?"

"If his stomach can wound him, bullets surely can," the first man said.

"We need to get out of here," another woman said.

Nnamdi leaned against the wall. He felt faint. "Yes," he said weakly. "There is no one else in the house. Get out!"

There was a mad rush for the stairs and that was when Nnamdi spotted Ruff Diamond. He was staring hard at Nnamdi.

"Do you need help?" Ruff Diamond asked.

Nnamdi nodded. He'd looked down and, though he saw no wound on his shadow skin, he saw a puddle of blood pooling at the heel of his left foot. The sight shocked him more than anything. Why hadn't he thought he could truly get hurt doing all this superhero stuff? But some part of him *had* seen all this as a game. *Am I going to die?* he wondered. Ruff Diamond was tall, but he was still only twelve years old. He could barely support Nnamdi. But it was better than nothing. Together, they lurched up the stairs. And as they moved, Nnamdi began to remember all that had happened when he'd gone down into that basement. He shivered.

"You're the Man, huh?" Ruff Diamond asked.

"Yes." He was glad to be pulled away from his thoughts. He'd taken on six men and one woman at once. In the struggle, he'd been shot in the leg. That's what the pain was.

"I thought you only protected Kaleria."

Nnamdi paused, remembering more. Mrs. Puneneh had shot him. He'd walked right up to her and grabbed her gun, crushed it with his bare hands, and then whacked her hard across the face with an open palm.

"Aren't you from Kaleria?" Nnamdi said. He rubbed his temples as he remembered more. He'd punched a man hard in the gut and slammed another against the wall like a dirty carpet, but he hadn't killed anyone. Then the hostages had rushed in and attacked the others.

"You came for me?" Ruff Diamond asked.

"Yes." No one in the room was dead. But how was that possible?

"All those other kidnapped people," Ruff Diamond said. "They are from other towns; three are even from Lagos! We need more people like you."

If there were more like me, who knows what would happen? he thought. *I barely even know what happens when there is one of me.* Nnamdi and Ruff Diamond stepped onto the driveway and found everyone was standing around, trying to decide how to get out of Tse-Kucha. Nnamdi fought to think clearly.

He'd freed these people; they were his responsibility. And if they didn't get out of here soon, Mrs. Puneneh's backup would arrive and recapture them all. Chioma, he had to get back to Chioma. And that's when he had the idea.

"Everyone," Nnamdi said. "I know how we can all get out of here. Follow me!"

Of course, they followed him.

"Your leg!" Chioma exclaimed. "You've been shot!"

"It's fine," Nnamdi said. His leg was aflame with angry pain, but Chioma didn't need to know this.

"Good," she said, looking at the people behind him. She nodded vigorously. "You did it! And you brought everyone!"

Nnamdi had to strain to speak because of the pain. "Yeah. I thought we could use—"

"I had the same idea, to bring them here," Chioma said. "We can all escape! I already put the keys in each car."

Within minutes, escaped hostages were starting cars all over the lot. They took the ones on the outside that could be most easily driven off. A few of them drove alone, but most drove in twos and threes. They drove away without a thank-you or a goodbye.

Ruff Diamond, the only kid among the hostages, stayed with Nnamdi. "There she is!" Ruff Diamond said, spotting Chioma. They ran to her and Nnamdi couldn't help grinning when he realized that she'd found the Mercedes. She and Nnamdi looked at each other for a long moment. Then Nnamdi nodded. There was no other way. Plus, they were the only ones heading back to Kaleria.

Chioma gave Ruff Diamond a hug. "Thank God you're okay," she said. Before he could ask, she added, "I'll explain in the car."

The three of them climbed in, Nnamdi in the driver's seat and Chioma in the passenger seat. Ruff Diamond got in the back and immediately locked the door.

"Why can't you just drive?" Nnamdi nervously asked.

"I would, but I'm small," she said. "My feet still don't reach the pedals that well. Trust me, it makes a difference. We need to do this fast; it'll be better if I guide you."

As the Man, Nnamdi was more than adult size. His long legs barely allowed him to squeeze into the driver's seat. "How do I turn on the car?" Nnamdi asked in his low voice.

"You can't drive?" Ruff Diamond exclaimed.

"Relax," Chioma said. "I know how to do it." She reached over and turned the key in the ignition. The car roared to life. The tank was nearly completely full. The thieves must have had special plans for Bonny's car. "Now, see the two pedals?" she told Nnamdi.

"Are you serious?" Ruff Diamond shouted. "There's no time to *learn* how to drive. We need to get the hell out of here! We got lucky in the house. But they're probably coming after us right now. Some of those guys are gonna hear these cars starting and driving off! They *will* kill us, trust me! All those guys care about is money."

"Can *you* drive?!" Chioma snapped.

"NO! But I'm not a goddamn adult!" he screamed. "HE is!"

Nnamdi turned around and looked Ruff Diamond squarely in the face. "No, I'm NOT!"

Ruff Diamond's jaw dropped open.

"It's Nnamdi, Ruff Diamond," Chioma said. "*He's* the Man. He's strong, but he's still twelve, like you and me! Nnamdi, that pedal is the brake and that's the gas. Got it?" She put the car in gear just as a bullet hit the windshield.

"*Kai!*" Ruff Diamond screamed, flattening himself on the back seat.

Nnamdi mashed his foot on the accelerator and they shot forward. The next shot hit the car behind them. He hit the brake and Ruff Diamond nearly flew into the passenger front seat with Chioma.

"Focus!" Nnamdi said aloud. "Focus!"

"Touch the accelerator *softly!*" Chioma screamed.

Nnamdi wrestled with the steering wheel as he lurched and drove the car around the other cars. He glanced in the rearview mirror. One of the men from the computer store was coming after them. He still had copper wiring on his arms and wrists, but he was aiming a gun at the car. Another three men were running into the lot from the other side, also with guns. The computer store guy was the most immediate danger. He was much closer and far angrier.

Nnamdi stamped his foot on the accelerator and they shot forward again as they drove around another car. A shot fired. He heard the bullet zoom past Chioma's window. Nnamdi gnashed his teeth, angry. It was one thing to shoot him; it was another to harm Chioma. He slammed on the brakes and opened the car door.

"Nnamdi!!" Chioma screamed. She grabbed the gearshift and put it in park. Nnamdi glanced at the car, noted that Chioma and Ruff Diamond were okay, and then started running. He was in that zone again, but this time he was aware of himself. He felt in control. He was in control of everything. Even his anger. He was doing this for Chioma. He ran at the man from the computer store, seeing him in tunnel vision tinged with red. The world slowed down around Nnamdi. But he moved faster. In the darkness, he saw all things clearly and he knew the computer guy could not see him because he was blacker than shadow, like a slice of outer space. All the computer guy with the gun probably saw was the car door opening.

Nnamdi closed the distance quickly and was on the man before he could fire another shot. He did all these things at once: grabbed and crushed the gun as he shoved the muzzle upward, grabbed the man's neck, shoved a knee into his gut, and growled deep, like a lion. They landed in the grass and

Nnamdi brought his shadowy face an inch from the man's face and roared, "You get up and you *die!!!*" The man coughed, cried, and curled into a ball like a wounded animal.

The other men had stopped where they were, staring as Nnamdi got up and stood tall. These were not the men who'd been in the house. These men most likely were not from Kaleria, so they knew little about the Man. And if they did, they certainly didn't expect him all the way in Tse-Kucha. Most of them probably thought they were seeing a shadow monster. *All the better to scare them straight,* Nnamdi thought.

"Change your ways," he bellowed in his deep voice. "Stop the evil that you do here. If you don't, I will come back and stop it myself. Go back to that house where the hostages were, see the men and woman who lie there. *That* is how I will do it." The man Nnamdi had attacked started crawling away, coughing and weeping. The other men just stood there staring at Nnamdi. He turned, returned to the car, and got in. In the rearview mirror, he could see Ruff Diamond staring at him.

"That was fantastic," Chioma said, grinning. She looked at Ruff Diamond. "Don't you think?"

Ruff Diamond only looked blankly at Chioma and then at Nnamdi's shadowy non-face. Chioma put the car into drive and Nnamdi gently pressed the accelerator. As they moved, Chioma reached for something on the floor of the back seat.

"There was a pickup truck full of these," she said, holding

up a huge red-green mango. "I threw some in the car while I was waiting for you." She tossed it at Ruff Diamond. He caught it and Chioma grinned wider.

Slowly and steadily, they drove off, leaving the confused, terrified men standing there.

16

Night Drive

"HOW'S YOUR LEG?" Chioma asked.

Nnamdi nodded, gritting his teeth. "I'm fine," he lied. "I think . . . I think it stopped bleeding, at least." That was the truth. And that was a good sign because, either way, there was nothing they could do about it. They needed to get home and he was the only one tall enough to properly drive the car.

The more Nnamdi drove, the easier it got. As soon as they were on the paved road, he even picked up a little speed. A little. He was going thirty-five miles per hour. Then forty. He knew the way out of town, but that was it. And it was dangerous to use his GPS power while driving. They needed to get directions. At this time of night, stopping would be risky, especially since he'd been shot.

"There," Chioma said, pointing at a small house beside the road where an old man was shuffling into the front door. He'd probably just come from the outhouse, for this house didn't look like it had running water or electricity. Chioma opened her window when they got closer and called out, "Sir!"

The old man turned around. As they pulled up next to him, Chioma said, "Sir, please. We need some help."

"It's late; you shouldn't be out," the old man said in a gruff voice. An old woman peeked out the door.

"You are correct," Chioma said. She paused and looked at Nnamdi. Then she turned back to the old man. "You live here and you are old," she said. "Elders always know what's happening. Haven't you seen cars speeding past your house in the last few minutes?"

The old woman now came out and stood beside the old man. "Shhh," she said. "Yes. We both have."

"What is going on?" the old man asked. "Have *they* escaped?"

"Yes," Chioma said.

"Oh, thank goodness," the old woman said.

"I'm one of them," Ruff Diamond said. "They took me from my mother. My father is very wealthy and they were trying to get him to pay a ransom."

"This country, o, so full of corruption. We need a hero like Kaleria has the Man," she said.

You have no idea, Nnamdi thought.

"That is interesting," Chioma said. "In Kaleria, they treat him like a criminal."

The old man was squinting through the window at Nnamdi, trying to get a closer look.

"That's where we need to go," Chioma quickly said. "Can you tell us how to get there?"

"I was born there," the old woman said. "That's a five-hour drive. Do you have enough fuel?"

"I don't know—"

"Who is this driving the car?" the old man asked. "Why doesn't he say anything?"

They all turned to Nnamdi. All looking at him, in his shadowy shape. Never had he felt so real. This was all actually happening. They were all *seeing* him. He was glad it was the middle of the night.

"He's the one who saved us all," Chioma said.

The old woman was delighted and pointed at Nnamdi. "Is he—"

"Yes," Chioma said.

"Would you mind if I used my mobile phone to snap your picture?" the old woman excitedly asked.

Nnamdi didn't know whether to smile or just sit there as the old woman took photo after photo of him. She'd look at her phone, frown, and take another. He didn't know why he'd agreed to be photographed. After several attempts, even with the light on in the car, the old woman finally gave up.

"He's not meant to have his picture taken," the old man said. He chuckled and nodded. "I could have told you it wouldn't work. But, my wife, you always have to see everything for yourself."

"I still think you deserve to have your picture taken," the old woman muttered.

Not only did the old couple tell them how to get back to Kaleria, but the old woman wrote it on a piece of paper and the old man gave them a jerrican full of fuel, some bottles of water, and more mangoes. Ruff Diamond was especially happy. He'd eaten the three that Chioma had put in the car and he was still hungry. He hadn't eaten in two days. Nnamdi and Chioma offered to give the old couple the rest of their money for the fuel, but they refused.

As they turned onto the main road, Chioma said, "It's always good to respect elders." She bit into a mango she'd peeled. The crescent moon hung low in the sky, barely lighting their way.

17

Home Is Kaleria

NNAMDI'S MOTHER OPENED the door, Bonny look-
ing over her shoulder. Her worn, red-eyed face lit up like the
sun. "NNAMDI!" she screamed, grabbing and yanking him
to her. She paused, holding him away from her and looking
at the blood on the leg of his pants. "What? Are you . . . ?"

"It's not . . . I'm fine," Nnamdi quickly said. "It was just
a scratch. The bleeding has stopped." When he'd turned
off the car in front of his mother's house and changed back
to himself, the first thing he did was pull up his pant leg.
He was afraid of what he'd see. Maybe it wasn't bleeding,
but there would certainly be a nasty hole. He could feel a
wound on both sides of his thigh, which meant the bullet
had gone through his leg. Right there in the car, the three
of them watched the dark red hole in his thigh close up.
It hurt horribly, but it was a small price to pay for healed
flesh.

Still hugging Nnamdi, his mother now looked up. She saw Chioma just as Chioma's parents came running down the hall from the living room.

"Nnamdi's back?!" Chioma's mother frantically asked. "Nnamdi's back? Is . . . CHIOMA!!!"

Chioma's mother picked Chioma up before her stepfather could get to her.

"Oh, Chioma," she said, hugging her tightly. She started sobbing. Chioma's stepfather threw his arms around them both.

"Oh my God! And Debo Okunuga!" Nnamdi's mother said, noticing Ruff Diamond. She pulled him to her with Nnamdi. Bonny held Nnamdi's hand, tears in his eyes, too.

"We brought back your car," Nnamdi told him, his mother's arm around his shoulders. There was a little blood on the seat from his leg and mango peels in the back seat. He held his breath as he watched Bonny run past him to go see.

Bonny slowed when he got to his car. He walked around it. Then he pumped his fists in the air and shouted, "Yes! Yes! Yes!" He turned to Nnamdi and grinned. Nnamdi grinned back, relieved. People came out of their homes to see what the shouting was about. Mr. Oke was off duty, but several people had seen Nnamdi, Chioma, and Ruff Diamond pull up to the gate in Bonny's car. And when they'd entered, they'd left the gate open.

"Oh, my beautiful son," Nnamdi's mother wept. "We all

thought the Man had taken you! Then you, Chioma Nwa-zota, sweet, sweet girl!" She turned to Ruff Diamond. "Your mother told me you'd been kidnapped. She wouldn't let me go to the police because she didn't trust them, but she thought I, of all people, would know what to do. We need to call her and your father immediately!"

After contacting Ruff Diamond's parents, she convinced them that it was all right to call the authorities. By noon, Nnamdi, Chioma, and Ruff Diamond found themselves sit-ting at a table face-to-face with Chief Okimba. They had dis-cussed and agreed on what they would tell the police. No one was going to believe the real story, so they had no other option—they had to demonize the Man by saying he had kidnapped Nnamdi. And in a way he had, during the days Nnamdi was in the abandoned school.

Nnamdi, who'd changed into a fresh T-shirt and shorts, wanted to slap Chief Okimba. He was exhausted from all that had happened and the drive through the night. He hadn't had a wink of sleep; his patience was running very low. Okimba reeked of expensive cologne and had heavily manicured fin-gernails, and the lines of his hair were shaved so sharp that his hair looked painted on. What kind of chief of police wore a huge diamond earring in each ear? He interviewed them individually. Nnamdi was last.

"Good morning, son," Chief Okimba said. They were alone in the kitchen. The chief dabbed his forehead; he was a big man, it was hot, and for some reason, he was wearing his full uniform, medals, beret, and all.

"Good morning," Nnamdi quietly replied.

"How are you feeling?"

"I'm alive."

"Well, it's good to see you that way instead of another way."

"Yes."

"You look like your father," he said. "Same eyes and chin. Looks like you'll be tall like him, too."

"I hope so, sir," Nnamdi said.

"Yes, well, let's hope when you get older, your claim to fame will be more than escaping from the Man," the chief said.

"Yes, sir," Nnamdi muttered.

"So he kidnapped you and the other two?"

"Yes."

"Why? Is he some sort of crazy man? Was he going to sell you? Use you as child slaves?"

Nnamdi shuddered. The media and authorities would not be kind to the Man. "I don't know why," Nnamdi said.

"Do you know his whereabouts?"

"No," Nnamdi said. "He . . . he is good at hiding."

"If we get someone here to draw him, can you describe his face?"

"No, sir," Nnamdi said. "He kept his face hidden very well."

"Ugh, why can't you kids be more useful? How is it that none of you saw the Man's face?!"

Nnamdi shrugged.

"Where did he keep you?"

"Um . . . it was dark when he took me, and he . . . uh, blindfolded me."

"Did he beat you?"

"No, I—"

"Did someone call the press?" Ruff Diamond shouted from the other room.

"I know I didn't," Chioma said. Nnamdi heard the front door open and then Chioma added, "Oh, you're kidding."

There was a knock on the kitchen door and Nnamdi got up and opened it.

"Did you call the press?" Chioma asked the chief, peeking in the kitchen. Ruff Diamond glared at the chief from over Chioma's shoulder.

"Well, not me, exactly," Chief Okimba stammered, looking away.

"Why?" Nnamdi asked Chioma.

"Look outside!" she said.

A crowd of people had come right through the open gate, passing Bonny's car. The house was now surrounded by journalists carrying cameras, hand devices, and notebooks. Some were already interviewing neighbors and some were filming the house, but most stood there waiting.

"Excuse me," the police chief said, getting up. He patted his perfect hair and tore off a paper towel from the roll on the counter. He dabbed his sweaty face and straightened out his uniform.

The chief, two of his constables, and the divisional police officer gave a press conference right on the steps of Nnamdi and his mother's house, with cameras flashing and microphones recording. Nnamdi stood behind them, frozen as Okimba called the Man a kidnapper and Kaleria's number one most wanted criminal. Nnamdi felt numb inside, but only because he needed a good ten hours of sleep. And the press conference wasn't the end of it. The editor in chief of the *Kaleria Sun* himself, Ikenne Kenkwo, sauntered in and walked up to Chief Ojini Okimba.

"Is this the boy?" he asked, glancing at Nnamdi. Nnamdi stepped forward to introduce himself, but then Kenkwo turned back to Okimba. Nnamdi felt his face heat with embarrassment. He balled his fists and pressed them to his sides.

"It is," Okimba said.

Kenkwo looked at Nnamdi again. But this time Nnamdi just looked away. Kenkwo chuckled and said, "Oh, he looks exhausted."

18

Plan

BONNY, CHIOMA, RUFF Diamond, and their parents, some neighbors, a few aunties and uncles and cousins, and a happy Mr. Oke (who'd returned to work when he heard of their return) all stayed at the house that night and a spontaneous celebration occurred.

As the highlife music played in the living room and palm wine, mineral, and other refreshments flowed, the exhausted Nnamdi retreated to the bathroom and took a long hot shower, his first in days. The water felt so good on his skin. *His* skin. Well, except for the still healing cut on his chest where Never Die had slashed at him and the raised bruise on his leg from the gunshot wound.

As he stood beneath the hot water, he shut his eyes and used his will to focus on what he knew was in him. *I have to be able to change whenever I want so I can do what I need to do*, he thought. Was he talking to the Man? To himself? He didn't know who he was addressing, but he knew that "who" was inside him and a part of him. It happened quickly and smoothly, his head softly bumping the showerhead. His heart slammed in his chest. And the warm water from the shower felt like wind. He immediately made it happen again. And within a second, he was back to his twelve-year-old self. He smiled, dunking his head into the hot shower stream.

"Show me," Chioma whispered.

After his shower, Nnamdi had dressed and gone to find Chioma. They were outside in the spot where Mr. Oke usually sat during the day. Now Mr. Oke was inside celebrating with everyone else. Ruff Diamond had had enough and gone to Nnamdi's room, where he was now fast asleep. Chioma sat in Mr. Oke's old leather seat.

Nnamdi looked around to make sure no one would see. Then he changed into the Man. It was so easy now. It had become a part of him. And though he felt a strong sensation of power and potential anger, he knew he could control and guide it.

Chioma stood and stared up at him. "Finally, I get to just look at you," she said. "You look . . . so . . . black." They both giggled. "And your voice sounds like a monster, all low and big-big." She imitated his laugh with a low voice as she walked around him, looking him up and down. "How do you *feel* when you're like this?"

"Like I could break a tree with my bare hands," Nnamdi said, holding them up. "And to do it would feel *good*. I feel like I could jump over a car, run through a brick wall, all this stuff."

"You feel like Superman, then?"

"More like the Hulk," he said.

"Who is the Hulk?"

Nnamdi only shook his head. He'd been trying to get Chioma to read his Hulk comics for years, but she was so not interested that any mention of the Hulk brought the same question.

"What happens to your clothes?" she asked, poking at his arm with her skinny finger. Nnamdi could barely feel it.

"Dunno. I guess they're underneath? When you found me and I changed back, my clothes where Never Die cut me were all ripped and dirty, remember?"

"Not really, wasn't paying attention," she said, touching and then rubbing at the skin of his arm. "You feel hot and kind of staticky, like the screen of my grandpa's old television." She pinched him. "Do you feel that?"

"Yes, Chioma," he said. "But only a little. When I got stabbed and shot, I felt everything. I'm not protected against pain."

She sat on the leather chair and Nnamdi changed back. "Wow," she whispered.

"Yeah."

"So . . . why would your father give you a power that is so dangerous?"

Nnamdi shrugged. He'd thought about this himself. "Daddy was a crime fighter," he said. "Maybe . . ."

Chioma nodded. "Maybe he wasn't done."

"And maybe he didn't want to see Kaleria in flames. Not even as a spirit. And maybe he didn't know exactly what would happen."

They were quiet for a moment. Nnamdi knew they were both remembering his father, but he didn't want to say any more. It made his heart heavy.

"Do you think we stopped it? You know, by going to Tse-Kucha and getting the car? And setting all those people free?"

Nnamdi shrugged. "I hope so. But there's more to do."

"Maybe . . . oh, I hate to say this, but . . . maybe we have to take down the Chief of Chiefs," Chioma suddenly said.

Nnamdi nodded. "Glad to hear someone else say what I've been thinking."

"But you and I have to do it, not just the Man," she added.

The smile dropped from Nnamdi's face.

"The ring. You said he had your father's ring."

"Yeah. The Chief of Chiefs was wearing it when he came to the funeral, the arrogant bastard." He felt the Man ripple deep inside him. The Man, always there, waiting and awake.

"Relax," she said, pinching her chin and narrowing her eyes. "Hmmm, well, let's start with the ring, then." She reached into her pocket and brought out a folded newsletter. "They ran this a few days ago. I kept it." She paused as Nnamdi read the announcement in the newsletter that Chioma had circled. The Chief of Chiefs would be having a banquet party in a week. "You were still missing and . . . I was going to try to get the ring."

"What?! Why?"

"To prove that he killed your father," she said. She shrugged, looking way. "It was a stupid idea . . . but I had to do *something*." Nnamdi raised his hands to hug her, hesitated, and instead patted her on the shoulder. She must have suffered so much when he was missing, with her world stuck in long shadows just as he was stuck as the Man.

"And why would a newsletter even report about the Chief of Chiefs' banquet? That's like free advertising," she said. "He's a known criminal."

"Those people," Nnamdi muttered. "They will report anything that sells newsletters."

Chioma jumped up and began pacing back and forth. Nnamdi pinched his chin, stretching out his legs. After a few minutes, they put their heads together and talked it out. Before long, they had a plan.

Ruff Diamond sat up in Nnamdi's bed, frowning deeply as he looked closely at Nnamdi.

"What are you two up to?" he finally asked.

"The less you know, the better," Chioma said.

"You're not going to kill anyone or anything, right?" he asked.

Nnamdi chuckled. "No."

"And you're not going to get yourself killed?"

"Hope not," Nnamdi said.

Chioma elbowed him. "No, we're not."

"Well, what if your mother calls?" Ruff Diamond asked.

"I'll tell her not to," Nnamdi said. "She'll just be happy I'm doing something normal after all that happened. And you can't get more normal than a sleepover." It was a risk, Nnamdi knew. There was indeed a strong chance that his mother *would* call. But if he assured her that he would be all right and his mother should call only if it were an emergency, things would be okay. As long as Ruff Diamond was willing to cover for him. Chioma's friend Onuchi had already agreed to cover for her.

Ruff Diamond squinted at Nnamdi and Nnamdi waited. Nnamdi could practically hear him thinking right now. He was probably trying to imagine Nnamdi as the Man again, as he turned all the details over in his head. Nnamdi hoped he didn't think too hard, because the plan was kind of risky.

"Okay," Ruff Diamond finally said. "I'll do it. No shaking."

19
Party

A WEEK LATER, Nnamdi and Chioma met up under the same streetlight where Nnamdi had initially met his father's ghost. Nnamdi got there before Chioma. As he looked around, his belly fluttered. He couldn't help looking for his father. But the only people in the area were some young men across the street, talking animatedly.

"Nice outfit," Chioma said as she stepped into the light.

"Do I look enough like a waiter?" He did a slow turn, showing off his white dress shirt, white pants, and white but dirty gym shoes.

She nodded. "How about me?" She was wearing navy-blue pants and a white blouse. She looked more like a student.

"Sort of," he said. "A waiter who is too young . . . I guess I do, too. But I don't think they'll notice." *Hopefully, not before we can get the ring*, he thought.

They pooled their naira. They had just enough to get

them to the banquet and back. Chioma hailed a taxi as if she'd done it a million times. "My mother has me do it when she has too many things to carry from the market," Chioma said as they got in.

The grandiose white mansion was surrounded by lush palm trees and a heavy white-bricked gate tipped with pointy wrought-iron designs. If they couldn't talk their way in, they'd be in trouble, because there was no way they could scale that gate. Nnamdi had stressed and stressed about how they would convince the gateman to let them in. What if it was obvious that he didn't know what he was talking about? What if Chioma started talking and said too much? What if their uniforms were wrong? Cars were packed into the large parking lot and crowded along the sides of the road outside the mansion. Those walking to the gate entrance were dressed in vibrant *ankara* dresses and suits, immaculately white agbadas, and *sokotos*. Flamboyant *geles* fanned from women's heads like satellites. Some wore complete three-piece designer suits and tuxedos.

Nnamdi and Chioma didn't say anything as the taxi dropped them off and sped away. Nnamdi felt sweat trickle down his back despite the fact that it was a mild night. He could grow into a tall shadow man with superhuman strength and fight off six men at the same time, yet here he was nervous about simply getting into the home of one criminal. Life could be so complicated. He reached into himself and felt the Man stir. Nnamdi smiled and stood up straighter.

"Let's hurry," Chioma said.

"Go in through the back" was all the gateman said when they walked up to make their case. They hadn't had to say a thing. And just like that, they were in.

The floors of the Chief of Chiefs' mansion were thick periwinkle marble, even in the kitchen. That was the first thing that caught Nnamdi's eye. His mother's favorite color was periwinkle. The second thing was that the kitchen was in organized chaos. Large pots of red stew, boiling rice, pepper soup, and *egusi* soup bubbled. The counters were packed with trays heavy with spicy skewers of suya and chin chin. The air was thick with heat and the spicy aroma of all kinds of delicious things. The Chief of Chiefs wasn't interested in Western foods like stuffed mushrooms and caviar.

Nnamdi had to admit he was a little surprised. His parents had often spoken of the dinner parties they had to attend that were held by "the Important People." They always returned late at night and Nnamdi would get up and join them as his mother would cook up a "real meal," as opposed to the "bland, tasteless dishes of the West" served at these parties.

Young servants moved in and out of the kitchen, setting down empty trays and grabbing fresh ones. Nnamdi and Chioma went to the door and took a peek down a grand flight of marble steps that led into the large backyard. Surrounded by tiki lights, the party was huge. Men in black suits or colorful traditional attire and women in all kinds of dresses milled about. At the back, a crowd of people danced as a band played an Afrobeat tune on a portable stage. The lead singer sported long, thick dreadlocks with blond tips. He grinned as he swung them about and sang a reggae song in Yoruba. To the right was a large buffet heavy with food. The line for it wound all the way around the party. People laughed, ate, danced. Nnamdi wondered how many of these people were criminals.

"Look over there," Chioma said, pointing. "Isn't that the chief of police? All the way near the back, where people are dancing."

"What?" Nnamdi squinted and then gasped. "No way!!" He was far off, but you couldn't miss the guy near the stage in the white caftan dancing spasmodically, graceless as an old chicken. He was surrounded by laughing women who wiggled around him, urging him to dance harder. Yes, that was him. Kaleria's chief of police was at the Chief of Chiefs' party, shamelessly getting down. Nnamdi's heart fell and he leaned against the doorway. A hand tapped hard on his shoulder and, when he turned around, a tray of chin chin was shoved to his chest.

"What are you standing around for?" a sweaty woman asked. She dropped a small silver spoon in the chin chin and gave Nnamdi a stack of green plastic plates. "Move, move, move!"

Before Nnamdi knew it, he was shoved toward the party. He turned around and met Chioma's eyes as the same woman dragged her toward the bubbling pots of stew. "I'll meet up with you later," Chioma said over her shoulder. "Find the ring."

How was he supposed to find anything in this madness? He walked down the stairs and, before he even made it to the grass, a tall elderly man came up to him, grabbed a plate from him, and used the spoon to scoop the sweet cookie-like bits onto his plate. He grunted, barely acknowledging Nnamdi as a human being, and put the spoon back on the tray. As he moved through the party, before Nnamdi knew it, his tray was nearly empty. He didn't have to say or do much; people treated him like a robot who didn't deserve even a hello or eye contact.

This was fine with Nnamdi because it allowed him to get a look around. His heart nearly leapt into his throat when he spotted the short old woman in the spectacular multicolored lace wrapper and matching top. Her gele was huge, which Nnamdi thought made her look even shorter. Nevertheless, despite her amazing outfit that Nnamdi knew all his aunties would go crazy over, the woman wore her signature black blocky shoes. Even without the shoes and expensive stylish outfit, Nnamdi would recognize Mama Go-Slow anywhere. When had *she* been released? He backed away and bumped into a tall man with muscles that wanted to burst from his suit. He was dark-skinned with vehicle tribal marks etched on his cheeks. He glared down at Nnamdi.

"Watch yourself, young man," he said in a deep voice.

"Sorry," Nnamdi muttered.

The man was about to say something else, but then his eyebrows went up with surprise. He smiled uncomfortably and backed away. A hand fell on Nnamdi's shoulder and squeezed. Nnamdi turned and found himself face-to-face with the Chief of Chiefs.

20

Long Live the Chief

WELL, TECHNICALLY, NNAMDI was not exactly face-to-face with the Chief of Chiefs. Nnamdi was taller. Nevertheless, the sheer presence of the man made him feel very small. Everything he wore was probably brand name, but Nnamdi wasn't well versed enough in brand names to know which ones. The Chief's fragrance probably would have impressed Chioma's sharp nose. Nnamdi felt everyone's attention suddenly shift, focusing on him and the Chief.

"Would you like some chin chin?" Nnamdi asked, offering a warm smile. If the Chief didn't recognize him, he'd be fine. He'd move on quickly and then quietly slip away to search for the ring in secret.

"Nnamdi Icheteka," the Chief said.

Nnamdi's eyes grew wide. "I'm . . . sir, I . . ."

"Why don't we find a nice quiet place to talk?"

"Oh . . . okay," was all Nnamdi could say. He felt pressure

on his bladder. He took a deep breath and the need to pee lessened. He would *not* urinate on himself from fear as he had when he'd met the Chief at his father's funeral.

It didn't surprise Nnamdi that the inside of the Chief's house was paradise. From the outside, he'd seen that it rose into four floors of large windows, solid brick, and marble. Several windows featured a door leading onto a balcony. The house looked simultaneously like a five-star hotel *and* a gateway into an African kingdom. But the inside was even more striking. The rooms looked like the home of a very old-fashioned yet modern-minded wealthy man. The house was a sprawling mansion that spread out on the ground like the palace of a king. The hallway they walked down was long and wide. Tribal masks and brass-framed African paintings hung on the walls. The air-conditioned air smelled like perfume.

"We can talk in my private study," the Chief said when they came to a pair of solid ebony doors. He opened one of the doors and motioned with his hand for Nnamdi to enter. Nnamdi glanced at the Chief's hand. There was the ring.

Like the heavy doors, the walls were made from dark polished wood, as was the desk near the wall-sized window. The Chief walked around the desk and sat in the dark red leather office chair, which creaked under his weight. The walls on his left and right were covered with filled bookshelves. Nnamdi spotted classics he'd heard older kids complaining about at his school, including Homer, Dante, and Shakespeare. But he also noticed African authors his mother liked to read, like Chinua Achebe, Nuruddin Farah, Flora Nwapa, and Christopher Okigbo.

"'His eyes grow large. Deep black eyes,'" the Chief of Chiefs recited, gazing at Nnamdi. He paused and then grinned. "That is the poet Okot p'Bitek, a visionary of our times. Do you enjoy literature?"

"Do . . . do comic books count?"

The Chief frowned, pressing his lips together. "No."

"Oh," Nnamdi said.

The Chief eyed Nnamdi silently for several moments, to the point where Nnamdi began to seriously consider fleeing. His skin prickled and his palms were sweating. He glanced at the door, hating himself at the moment. He was the Man; why should he fear this small, small man . . . this man who had killed his father? He frowned and took a deep breath to steady himself. He was here for the truth, to get the evidence. He would get all of it.

"So, tell me," the Chief said. "What brings the ex-chief of police's son to dine with thieves?"

"I was not 'dining,'" Nnamdi said. "I was—"

"Do you have any idea how many dangerous people are here at my home on this fine night? Do you know how many people here walk around with blood on their hands?" the Chief said, his voice rising. "I have many young female servants. I've had to hire undercover guards to make sure that none of them disappear tonight. There are kidnappers, murderers, car thieves, terrorists, arsonists, money launderers, 419 scammers . . . Every type of criminal you can think of is here tonight eating, drinking, watching. And your father put many of these people in jail at one time or another. So I ask you again, what the hell are you doing here? It's not safe for you."

Nnamdi opened his mouth and then closed it. The Chief's concern for his well-being was confusing him. He frowned. He *had* to say something. If he didn't do it now, he'd kick himself for the missed opportunity later. *Talk, Nnamdi*, he told himself. *Come on!* The words came from deep within him, where the Man and his anger quietly boiled and mingled. "*You're* a murderer!" Nnamdi growled.

The Chief gazed at him as Nnamdi walked up to his desk and put his hand on it. Nnamdi leaned forward. "You may not be in jail, but I know the truth. Arrogant man. You're even wearing my father's ring as some sort of a sick trophy!" Tears welled in his eyes and he could feel his body wanting to change. *Good*, he darkly thought. *This way I will avenge Daddy's death with my bare hands and no one will know it was me.*

The Chief was calm as he watched Nnamdi closely.

"You have your father's eyes," he said, suddenly looking very serious and grave.

Nnamdi said nothing. He could smell it on the Chief: the

fierce control, confidence, and certainty in his actions. He could see why this small man was able to control so many corrupt people.

"Why would I want to kill your father?" he asked in a soft voice.

Nnamdi blinked, even more confused. Not "I didn't kill him," but "*Why* would I want to kill him?" The question was so odd that Nnamdi stepped back. Slowly, he sat down in a nearby chair. All the tension left his body. He felt so tired. "What?" Nnamdi asked.

The Chief opened a drawer on his side of the desk and brought out a chewing stick. Nnamdi shivered. His father loved chewing sticks, too. And he did the same thing; he kept a whole bunch in his side drawer. The Chief put his chewing stick between his lips and began to chew while watching Nnamdi.

Nnamdi could feel the Man just under his skin, trying to push forward again, muddling his brain and swelling his appetite for violence. He strained, holding the Man back.

"What is eating you?" the Chief asked.

Nnamdi closed his eyes and shook his head.

"Nnamdi, I did not kill your father."

Nnamdi opened his eyes. The Chief continued munching on his chewing stick and settled back in his chair. "Your father and I . . . we were childhood friends."

"Liar," Nnamdi spat. "My father—"

"Shut up and listen," the Chief snapped, clasping his hands in his lap. "You came here for a reason, that's clear. I will give you something better. Listen first and then decide what you want to do."

Yes, which will be to kill you, Nnamdi thought, his eyes burning with tears.

"Your father and I knew each other since we were little boys. We grew up on the same block, our mothers were best friends, and our fathers worked in the same insurance office. And we always had the same taste for justice."

He picked another chewing stick from his drawer and threw it at Nnamdi. It landed right in Nnamdi's lap. "Chew, it will calm you down. It's a habit your father taught me."

Nnamdi felt light-headed as he looked down at the chewing stick. A memory popped into his head. He had earned a poor grade on a math test and, not wanting to sit and wait all evening for his father to come home and punish him, he'd gone to see his father in his police station office. He'd sat in the chair across from his father while his father looked at the math test. Nnamdi hadn't studied and this was the result. His father had frowned, opened a desk drawer, and taken out a chewing stick. He chewed and chewed for several minutes before looking up at Nnamdi and calmly saying, "This is the worst thing I've ever seen. I don't want to see anything like it again." From that point on, Nnamdi had always earned strong grades in not only math classes, but all his classes.

Slowly, Nnamdi picked up the chewing stick the Chief had thrown at him. He placed it in his mouth and started chewing.

"Your father and I were born with it, that taste for jus-tice," the Chief repeated. "We wanted to leave the world a better place than when we came into it. Even from a young age we felt this way. But when we grew up, well, we chose different paths. He took the high road into the police depart-ment and I took the low road into the underground, trying to solve, or at least control, problems from the inside. But our paths both led to the same place—justice." He paused. "Nnamdi, I may look like the kingpin of Kaleria's crime ring, but I'm a revolutionary just as dedicated to helping Kaleria as your father. Corruption is systematic. . . . Your father's goal was to stamp it out while mine was to channel it as much as I could."

Nnamdi chewed his stick down to soft splinters and, as the Chief spoke, he threw Nnamdi another one. This one was mint flavored.

"Almost all those people out there, I manage them so at least they are not as bad as they could be. And I am like Robin Hood: I steal from the rich and give to the poor," he said. "For example, I anonymously donate millions of naira to schools and hospitals. Take that abandoned school building on the other side of town." He hissed, looking irritated. "That's one of my greatest failures. Those two American Nigerians in charge of it would not have raised even a wall of that school if it weren't for *me*. That was really *my* project. But I had to let it go when I learned those two planned to convert the school into a town shopping center as soon as it was finished. It was a bad business deal, so I shut it down."

Nnamdi pressed his fingers to his face, his head beginning to ache. Those American Nigerians were really going to do that? Why? And the Chief stealing from the rich and giving to the poor? This was criminal activity, no matter how honorable he made it sound. But in Kaleria, where even the police department could be corrupt, how else could one make things better? His father had tried in the legal way and he was killed for it.

"Your father was the only uncorrupted person in the department," the Chief of Chiefs said. "The sheer will of the people got him nominated for police chief, but I had to pay off key people in the department to get him the win."

Nnamdi felt sick. His father's election as the chief of police had only happened because of the same corruption he was fighting.

"You don't agree with my ways," the Chief said.

Nnamdi hesitated, but then slowly shook his head. "Crime . . . is crime."

The Chief chuckled and nodded. "You are your father's son. He never agreed either. Many times he and I argued and threatened each other. *He* believed wholly in justice and *I* could never believe that justice could ever be truly served under a corrupt system." He held up his hand. "But see this ring?"

"Yes," Nnamdi whispered.

"Your father had one and I have one," he said. "We bought them together when he entered the police force. We wanted something to help us stay connected since we knew we could not be close friends anymore. He was going to be police and I was moving up in the crime ring. This is the Ouroboros, the serpent eating its tail. It's an ancient African symbol that means 'life out of death.' *Kaleria* is the Ouroboros, feeding on itself because of its corruption. Aside from dedicating our lives to fight for justice in Kaleria, that was one thing your father and I agreed on." He laughed.

"One man gives money to build roads; another man eats the money so he can buy a Mercedes. One man gives money to help the schools; another man puts the money into his own bank account and calls the teachers thieves. Your father and I wanted to change this. We just didn't agree on the method."

He grew serious and sighed. "Nnamdi, on the last day that I saw him . . . alive, the night before his death, we met. You remember that? They reported it in the newsletter."

"Yes," Nnamdi said.

"We made an exchange. The newsletter only reported part of the story. It said that I was going to cooperate with your father to help stop the highway robberies in Kaleria that had gotten out of hand. Really, we were planning to work together to finally cure Kaleria of its corruption for good! I was willing to try. We were going to combine his method and mine."

"So who killed my father, then, if not you?"

"I am still trying to solve that mystery," the Chief said darkly. "When I do, that person will be handled."

Nnamdi's head was full as he and Chioma sat in the taxi. Chioma had listened intently as he told her all that had happened and then she said, "Let's just get out of here."

Nnamdi agreed. They were no closer to finding his father's killer, but he'd learned something just as valuable and he wanted to chew on that for a bit, away from the party full of criminals. The Chief of Chiefs wasn't his father's murderer; he was nearly his best friend, his closest colleague. Nnamdi leaned back and rubbed his forehead.

They carried large containers of food—jollof rice with goat meat, fried plantain, egusi soup, and chin chin. Chioma was happy to take the large plastic containers. "We earned them!" she'd laughed. Not only had she stirred her share of stew, rice, and soup, she'd walked all over the party with five trays of suya and chin chin and had even been asked to dance onstage. "It was great!" Chioma had told Nnamdi when he finally found her. Nnamdi was glad she'd at least enjoyed herself, despite the highly dangerous environment.

The taxi dropped them near her friend Onuchi's house and they parted ways. Nnamdi tapped on Ruff Diamond's bedroom window and Ruff Diamond let Nnamdi slip into his room.

"Jesus, it's eleven; I nearly died with worry!" Ruff Diamond said. "I had to watch *three* movies really loudly so that my mother wouldn't interrupt us!"

"Sorry," Nnamdi said.

Ruff Diamond looked him over. "Are you all right?"

Nnamdi nodded. "Just a lot on my mind. We got what we needed."

"Good," Ruff Diamond said, climbing back into bed.

"Aren't you going to ask me what we got?"

"No," Ruff Diamond simply said. He shook his head. "No." They paused, looking at each other. Then they both laughed.

Nnamdi lay on his side of Ruff Diamond's bed and was glad when his friend started snoring. He didn't think he'd sleep a wink. The Chief of Chiefs was not his father's murderer? He rolled this question around in his head, replaying their meeting over and over. Each time, he paused to remember the Chief of Chiefs using the chewing stick to think. *That* was the strongest evidence that he was telling the truth. The fact sunk into him. The Chief of Chiefs was not his father's murderer. *So who is?* Nnamdi wondered. And what was he fighting for if Kaleria was so hopeless that the only way to do good and *live* was to do some bad, like the Chief of Chiefs?

Nnamdi wanted to keep being the Man. He'd decided this as soon as Chioma had found him in the abandoned school and helped him get ahold of himself. But could he simply fight crime in Kaleria? Protect the people of Kaleria with no hope of truly cleaning it up? Simply make things better than they could have been, like the Chief? What if he never found out who shot his father? If even the Chief couldn't solve the mystery, could Nnamdi do any better? He shut his eyes tightly, his head pounding from thinking too hard about who it could possibly be. He rested his head on his pillow and quickly fell into a fitful sleep, his mind still turning the question over and over. *Who shot Daddy?*

As the sun rose, he sat up, realizing something he was sure was profound: He knew exactly who his father's murderer was. It was the only man he knew who had good reason to want his father out of the way—Bonny, his mother's boyfriend. *Why didn't I see it before?* he groggily thought. *It's so obvious.* Without waking Ruff Diamond, he got up, threw his street clothes on over his pajamas, and ran home.

21

Bonny's Head

NNAMDI WAS RUNNING.

He ran past houses where men and women polished their shoes outside, preparing for work. He ran past *agege* bread hawkers who sold bread and cheap butter. He saw everything, but greeted no one. His blood was burning and his head was pounding. He couldn't speak even if he wanted to. How had he not figured it out earlier?

He had to hurry. Bonny usually picked his mother up and drove her to work these days. Bonny, the man who'd killed his father in order to have his mother all to himself. Yes, it was so obvious. Nothing else made sense. Breathing hard, Nnamdi stopped and, right there in broad daylight on the side of the road, he shifted into the Man. He catapulted off, taking a back road. Not because fewer people would see him, but because it was faster. As the Man, he could quickly scale fences and jump over parked cars.

Bonny was in for trouble. *Oh, if he only knew,* Nnamdi

thought with focused anger. Nnamdi wanted him dead! How could a man kill another man, then turn around and woo the man's widowed wife? *Abomination!* Nnamdi's mind was beginning to cloud. He remembered how his father used to shout *abomination!* when he told his mother about the latest criminal deed he'd learned about at the police department. Nnamdi's anger exploded and he ran faster, leaping over two goats standing in the middle of a small path behind a house. Bonny had to die and his mother had to be saved from smiling into the eyes of an evil man, from loving him.

Vaguely, Nnamdi felt tears stinging his eyes and drying on his cheeks as he ran. *How did I not see Bonny's selfish, evil motive?* he wondered. *I was such a fool!* He slowed down when he arrived at the back of his compound. He heard Bonny's voice inside the gate, near the house. He ran around to the front, where the gate was open, and peeked inside. And there was the devil.

"Ezinne, hurry," Bonny was saying as he put the last of his mother's packages in the back of his Mercedes. "I want to buy some buns before I drop these things off!"

It was Saturday and Mr. Oke was off duty. Nnamdi was glad. He didn't know what he'd do to him if he tried to stop Nnamdi from doing what he was about to do. A fresh pulse of anger shot through his body. He grasped the side of the gate and squeezed. There was a satisfying crunch as the tips of his fingers bit into the metal.

His mother came running out of the house with one

last box full of yams. She was wearing the dress Bonny had bought her last week. His mother was growing lax. Now she was accepting more gifts from him. Nnamdi frowned. He frowned deeper as his mother took Bonny's hand and they both laughed, looking into each other's eyes.

"Thanks for doing this," she said. "Tell Fifi that I will join her as soon as my son gets home. She'll be in charge of the stall till then."

"That's what you pay her for," he said, hugging her close. "I'm proud of you, Ezinne. Your stall is doing so well."

His mother beamed.

Nnamdi was disgusted. He'd seen enough. It was time to pounce on his father's killer. Bonny was approaching the open gate, right toward where Nnamdi hid. He was going to push the gate wider. Nnamdi's sharp eyes narrowed as he calculated how many more steps the murderer had to take before he would grab him. Two steps, one step. *Come, Mr. Bonny,* Nnamdi thought. Closer and closer to Nnamdi he came. Closer and closer to the Man. Closer and closer to his death.

Nnamdi saw it at the very last moment. A thin white line of smoke surrounded Bonny's head. He froze as Bonny grasped the edge of the gate and pushed it wider. Then something that had never happened before happened. "Oh," he whispered. Nnamdi felt rather than heard the low, muffled voice in his mind. It calmly said, "Where there is smoke, there is no killer."

Nnamdi looked around, but he saw no one. "Who's there?" The back of his neck prickled. No answer. Then, not far from Bonny as he walked to his car, Nnamdi glimpsed . . . his father's dashiki, the long flowing robe he wore only on weekends. A near invisible glint of it. His mouth fell open. The cloth grew shadowy and, as Nnamdi squinted to get a better look with his extra-sharp eyes, it vanished. Now Bonny was in his car, waving goodbye to his mother. Nnamdi moved behind the wall so that Bonny wouldn't see him as he backed out.

The thin white line of smoke surrounded the car now. The gate banged shut as his mother closed it and Nnamdi sat on the concrete, all his power and anger leaving him. He covered his face with his hands. *His* hands . . . he'd changed back, the Man leaving him like helium from a balloon. "Oh God," he whispered. He'd nearly attacked an innocent man. Someone his mother cherished. Now that his mind was clear, he felt so ashamed. He'd been so desperate for an answer to his father's death that he'd thought something terrible about a good person.

Bonny would never have done such a thing. And his mother dating her husband's killer? She'd never ever be so easily manipulated. Nnamdi had been manipulated, by his own irrational need for justice. *Daddy, why did you give me this power?* he thought with his eyes closed. *Take it away. PLEASE.* He wiped sweat from his brow and tried to think.

If Bonny did not kill his father, then who had? He wished his father would just *tell* him.

He entered the house, greeted his mother, and went right to his room, hoping and hoping. He opened the pencil case. It was still in there. The Ikenga. His burden. His responsibility. His.

22

Determination

NNAMDI PACED HIS room, thinking and thinking and thinking. He'd helped his mother bring two huge pots of yam porridge to church for a small baptism celebration and now she was off to her stall. He wished he could go out and have a relaxing Saturday afternoon with friends, too. Ruff Diamond, Jide, Hassan, and some other kids were playing soccer in the field nearby. Chioma was also out there, chatting with some friends. But his mind was too occupied and bothered to allow him to go out and enjoy the nice day.

The Chief of Chiefs had denied killing his father and Nnamdi believed him. He seemed to be far more than he appeared. One day, Nnamdi planned to learn more about the Chief of Chiefs and his relationship with his father. Did his mother know of it? He didn't think so. The day she saw him at the funeral, she'd looked like she wanted him dead, too. However, before he could fully understand the mystery of the

Chief of Chiefs and his father, he had to solve the mystery of his father's death. The spirit of his father had told him that Bonny was innocent.

So why couldn't he just tell Nnamdi who did it? "Because Daddy wants me to figure it out on my own," Nnamdi whispered. "Oh, Daddy, why couldn't you have given me a super-brain to solve this? Instead, you gave me . . ." He punched his pillow, got up, and trudged to the bathroom. A pink wall gecko stood in the corner near the window. It had nabbed a large mosquito. Nnamdi stared up at it for a moment and then, despite himself, he smiled at the tiny aggressive creature.

"Well done," he said, chuckling. He turned on the tap and washed his face. The cool water felt good on his burning eyes. He was drying his face, still thinking and thinking, when his mind paused on the word *chief.* He pressed the towel to his face, rolling the word over in his mind. Over and over.

"Chief?" Nnamdi said to himself. "But the Chief of Chiefs didn't do it." He paused and then the thought bloomed in his mind like the answer to a math problem he'd been stuck on. "Oh!" he said. He shoved the towel untidily on the rack and dashed out of the bathroom. He threw on some shorts, a shirt, and some shoes, and for the second time in twenty-four hours set off running along the side of the street.

He knew who it was now. The one who killed his father was none other than the one man who took the most and the biggest bribes in Kaleria. He liked to appear on television and talk tough. He was a showman. He pretended to fight crime but he was corrupt. He'd even been at the Chief of Chiefs' party, dancing like a beer-soaked monkey. His father's successor. And he *was* a chief! The *new* chief of police! Chief Ojini Okimba.

Slowly, he stopped running. The police station was a ten-minute walk from his house. Unless he took a *kabu kabu*—he had enough money for one of those. He could change into the Man and make it in less than half the time, but it was broad daylight and thus too risky. He paused, considering everything as people around him enjoyed their Saturday. The afternoon was cool with a nice breeze. Kaleria was a good place to live, if only there were no criminals as well as a new police chief who protected criminals.

Chief Ojini Okimba's activities during his father's burial flashed through Nnamdi's mind as he walked to the street. He remembered Okimba's speech at his father's funeral, where he'd practically blamed his father for getting shot. Okimba had said, "In his next life, such a fine police officer will know better." Nnamdi shivered with anger at the memory. He held up a hand to hail a kabu kabu. *What kind of man says that in a speech at a police chief's funeral?* he wondered.

A kabu kabu slowed in front of him, but Nnamdi was still deep in thought. He had never heard of Okimba before he became the new chief of police, so he had no idea what his relationship had been like with his father. However, it was clear to Nnamdi that Okimba had had good reason to kill his father. Chief Okimba was known for taking bribes and dabbling in corruption; now he was living the good life with Nnamdi's father out of the way. Once Nnamdi got to the police station, he would force Okimba into a jail cell, lock him up, and escape with the keys. And if he refused arrest, he would *deal* with him. The Man already had a bad reputation; people expected him to behave that way. And they would never find and arrest Nnamdi, because he was the Man.

As he reached for the kabu kabu's rusty door handle, he felt his hands go clammy. He was being as irrational as he had been when he'd gotten stuck as the Man in the abandoned school. Hadn't he learned his lesson about what happens when you let anger cloud your mind? This wasn't the way to do it. *Maybe I should wait until night*, he thought.

Irritated, the kabu kabu driver cranked opened his cracked window and shouted, "Wetin come be dis kin nonsense? Why u mek me stop if you no dey go?" He angrily drove off, leaving Nnamdi in a wake of dust.

That night his mother and Mr. Bonny decided to go out to a restaurant. Mr. Oke also happened to be off duty. It was the first time Nnamdi was allowed to stay home alone. *What perfect timing*, he thought.

"I'll be fine," Nnamdi said as they left.

"You know where the mobile phone is?" his mother asked.

"Yes, Mommy."

"I'll call when we get to the restaurant," she said.

"No need," he said. "Send a text and I'll text you back."

Mr. Bonny laughed. "Let him be a man, Ezinne."

Nnamdi's mother kissed him on the cheek and went out-side. Bonny took him aside. "You sure you're okay with this?" he asked. "After the kidnapping and all?"

Nnamdi nodded.

"You're the son of a police chief, so you know more than anyone what's out there."

In that moment, Nnamdi truly began to like Bonny.

"If you want to come with us, that would be just fine. I'll tell your mother that I insisted," he said.

"Thanks, Mr. Bonny," Nnamdi said. "But I can do this. Really."

Bonny nodded and smiled. "I know you can." He patted Nnamdi on the shoulder. "And I'm glad you didn't take me up on my offer. You're a good kid, Nnamdi."

"Thanks, Mr. Bonny."

As soon as they were gone, Nnamdi ran into the night. It was a seven-mile run and a warm night, but as the Man, Nnamdi felt invincible and the heat brought not a drop of sweat to his shadowy body. He could run nearly as fast as the cars and, in the darkness of the night, no one could see him. He ran past the akara lady. He passed the closed market. Finally, he arrived at the police station.

He stopped at the steps that led up. He hadn't been here

since before his father died. He and his mother used to stop by to see him when he worked late. They'd bring him dinner. His office was full of stacks of paper and his telephone was always ringing. He kept a photo of his garden on the wall beside the framed image of the Nigerian flag and map of Kale-ria. *But it's not Daddy's office anymore*, Nnamdi thought. And right now, he wasn't Nnamdi, he was the Man.

He walked up the steps. He knew exactly where the office for the police chief was located. And he knew that the police chief usually worked late nights. Nnamdi also knew that the department building would be near empty.

He was barely at the front door when it opened and a tall woman in the tightest jeans Nnamdi had ever seen and an even tighter red blouse came out of the building. She wore super-high platform pumps with what looked like diamonds in the heels. Nnamdi only noticed this because they sparkled in the building's bright lights.

"Good evening, shadow man," she said to him in a smooth, buttery voice, without so much as a glance his way. She chuckled throatily as she quickly walked down the stairs.

"Good evening," Nnamdi said in his gruff voice. She was gone before he could worry about her noticing that he was more shadow than human being. How could she move that quickly down all those stairs in those shoes? he wondered. Still, he was glad she was gone. He went inside.

To Nnamdi's relief, the building was empty. He ran down

the hall, straight to the police chief's office. The light was on. The chief was in. Nnamdi took a deep breath. His mind was getting cloudy. He was seeing his father behind those doors. Alive. Less than a year and a half ago. Before the man who was now behind the door had had him killed or done it himself. Taken his father from him. He shuddered, thinking about the pain his father must have felt when he was shot, the loss as his life drained away from his chest and neck.

"I'll get him, Daddy," he said to himself. "I promise you." His voice was like thunder.

When he grasped the doorknob, Nnamdi was full of damage. He tore the brass knob out and kicked the door in. "GET READY TO DIE! YOU . . ."

There was no scream of fright. There was nothing. Nothing but . . . Nnamdi frowned and fought with himself to relax. The ringing in his head slowly died down. The throb of his heartbeat in his ears decreased. Silence. He listened. Someone was breathing. Loudly. Snoring?

He glanced around the office. The walls were bare, the pictures his father kept on the wall gone, leaving dark outlines where they'd been. Okimba had barely moved in nor had he had the place cleaned up. The desk was heavy with stacks of papers, with several more stacks on the floor. Nnamdi frowned. The snoring was coming from behind the desk. He peeked over it and nearly cried out.

There was the new chief of police, Chief Ojini Okimba,

sitting on a chair, fast asleep, with the word *Rubbish* written on his forehead in red lipstick. Nnamdi had kicked the door down and shouted and Okimba hadn't woken. His head was back and his mouth was wide-open as he loudly snored. His arms and legs were tied together with strong red rope. A note was taped to his chest.

"What the—" Nnamdi couldn't believe his eyes. "Chief Okimba!" he shouted.

The chief twitched and sluggishly opened his eyes. When he saw Nnamdi, his eyes grew wide and he screamed. Then he tried to bounce himself away, nearly capsizing the chair. "Blease! Ah, ah. Don' 'urt me, o!" he said, slurring his words. "Sh' took ever'ting!"

"Who?" Nnamdi shouted. "What happened here?!"

Okimba shut his eyes and shook his head. Then it seemed to dawn on him. "Are you the Man?"

"What happened here?" Nnamdi demanded.

Okimba seemed to become more alert as Nnamdi spoke. He started to talk. "'You're the chief of police,' she said. 'You should be kind enough to help me,' she said."

"What are you talking about?"

"I'm not even usually *here* late like this," he said hysterically. "I have a life, a family."

Nnamdi kissed his teeth.

"She stopped me as I was going to my car," Okimba continued. "That woman. Okay, so yes, she happened to be quite beautiful . . . but that wasn't why I tried to help her."

Nnamdi rolled his eyes. What a liar. Obviously, the woman being beautiful was *the* reason Okimba had paid any attention to her.

"She said she had no money to get home and buy food," Okimba continued. "She was appealing to my sense of decency, you see. I brought her here to . . . get her some cash."

Then Nnamdi understood. The chief of police had just been robbed. He blinked again, realizing more. He'd been robbed by the woman Nnamdi had seen coming out of the station minutes ago!

"She called herself Darling," Okimba said. "She must have put a sweetie in my beer that made me sleep."

"Why were you drinking beer with her?" Nnamdi asked. "In your office?"

"What does that matter? She took everything I had! My watch, my wedding ring. She sat here on my computer and transferred all the money in my bank accounts to some other account! Oh my *God*, I am ruined, o! God is punishing me, o!"

Nnamdi reached forward and plucked the note from his chest. He read it out loud: "I am Darling, but I am also fearless! See what I did to the chief of police! HA!"

"Oh God of Abraham," Okimba moaned. "Who wants to be a victim to something like this?! I'll be the laughingstock of Kaleria. I didn't even *want* the position of chief of police. No one else would step up after Egbuche Icheteka was shot."

Nnamdi froze. "You didn't want to be the chief of police?"

"Of course not!" he said. He cocked his head. "Do . . . do

you? Would you like to have the job? It doesn't pay well but it pays." He looked away. "No, *you* don't like the law, do you? What . . . what are you anyway? A ghost? Spirit? Demon?"

Nnamdi blinked, processing Okimba's words. Okimba wasn't the murderer either. It was time to go. "What am I?" Nnamdi asked, trying to sound as scary as possible. "I am always watching you. So do your job. My fa—Chief Icheteka would never have allowed something like this to happen."

"At least untie me, before you leave."

Nnamdi turned away. "I'll send you help."

"No, untie me now! You think I want anyone finding me like this? You leave me here . . . and I will tell everyone that it was *you* who robbed me. There are cameras on the building that will have shown you entering!"

Nnamdi had forgotten about the camera. His father had told him the same thing. The station was monitored twenty-four hours a day with cameras. Would he show up? He didn't know. He wasn't sure! Maybe? *Idiot, Nnamdi, idiot!* He wanted to smack his head. But did it really matter so much when everyone already thought the Man was a kidnapper of children? And who was to say that Okimba would not still accuse him even if he did untie him? Nnamdi turned and left. After alerting some of the bewildered-looking night-shift officers to what was happening in the police station building, Nnamdi got out of there quickly.

❤ ❤ ❤ ❤

In the morning, Nnamdi held his breath when he went out to get the paper. He hadn't stopped by Chioma's bedroom window to tell her what had happened. If the incriminating lies the chief threatened to tell were inevitable, what good would it do to discuss things with Chioma?

Now, newsletter in hand, he walked back home. He went to the back of the house and sat down in the middle of the garden. It was peaceful and quiet here, the air smelling of leaves, flowers, and soil. He'd replanted the sunflowers and vegetables. The yam may have been mashed, but the vine was at least still green and intact. Already, it was starting to shoot out a fresh pair of light green leaves at the tip. He opened the paper.

The headline read in big block letters, "ROBBED!" Right below it was a huge photo of a snoring chief of police slumped in a chair with the word *Rubbish* lipsticked on his forehead and a note taped to his chest as Darling stood beside him posing like a runway model. She wore a smiling masquerade mask to hide her face. Nnamdi burst out laughing and couldn't stop for the next ten minutes.

It turned out that Nnamdi had nothing to worry about, for the criminal calling herself Darling had sent an envelope full of photos along with a copy of the letter she'd taped to the chief's forehead. The chief was going to be so, so embarrassed when he saw the article, and the thought of this sent Nnamdi into another fit of laughter.

So Chief Okimba was innocent, too. *At least of murder-ing my father*, Nnamdi thought. *He's probably guilty of a lot of other things, like taking bribes and turning a blind eye to what certain criminals do.* Nnamdi folded and refolded the newslet-ter. Doing this helped him focus. He put the tiny triangle of newsletter in his pocket and took a deep breath. *What next?* he asked himself. He went for a walk. He'd mistaken three people as murderers so far. He needed to clear his head before he made another plan or move.

It was Sunday and plenty of people were out and about, enjoying the cool sunshine. As he walked, his eyes were drawn to two women a few yards away, standing in the shade of a building . . . both quietly reading newsletters. He looked around. A *lot* of people were reading them. Some were even walking beside the dangerous road as they read. The guy who ran the paper, the editor, he had people's minds in his hands with that newsletter. Nnamdi remembered the unpleasant interview he'd had with the newsletter's editor. The man was like a vampire.

Calmly, he turned and started walking the other way. He would not need a kabu kabu. He'd rather walk in the pleasant sunshine. The *Kaleria Sun*'s headquarters were farther than the police station, but Nnamdi had the time and he certainly had the energy.

"Nnamdi!" Chioma said a minute later as he passed near

her house. She'd just come out and was locking the door. Nnamdi smiled and waved. She joined him, hoisting up the small backpack she always carried. She was carrying a copy of the newsletter, too.

"I was just going to look for you," she said. "I have an idea. Have you ever noticed that the newsletter . . ."

They stared at each other, the unspoken flying between them in a way it only did between true friends. They'd realized it at the same time.

"Yes," Nnamdi finally said.

"We both go."

"You don't have to," he said. "I can handle him by myself."

"That's what I'm afraid of," she said knowingly. "I also was looking for you because I noticed the shadows starting to grow again."

Nnamdi nodded but said nothing. All he wanted to do was go. No more talking.

They walked for a few minutes in silence. Chioma looked at Nnamdi. "Why don't we take a kabu kabu or the bus?"

Nnamdi shook his head. "Trust me, the long walk is good for me."

"Oh," Chioma said, glancing at him. "I see. Then we walk." She smiled nervously. "Yes, let's walk. It's best to go into stressful situations with . . . a cool head."

They walked for a few more minutes, Chioma continually shooting glances at Nnamdi. Nnamdi focused on the sunshine and the warm breeze. He flared his nostrils and inhaled. As they walked, his nerves calmed. Chioma's presence had an additional calming effect.

The building was made of solid concrete and surrounded by a wrought-iron fence.

"Do you have any blank paper in your backpack?" he asked Chioma.

"Of course," she said. She reached in and brought out a notebook. Nnamdi smiled.

"That's perfect," he said. "A pen, too?"

She handed him one. The ink was pink.

"Okay, so we are two students who write for the school newspaper. We are doing a story on the editor in chief. We think he is the best journalist on earth and our story will be about why this is so true."

Chioma's face lit up. "Oh! With his huge ego, he'll have them bring us right in so we can interview him."

"Exactly."

The plan worked perfectly. The editor in chief, Ikenne Kenkwo, told the guard to send them right in. Within two minutes Nnamdi and Chioma were walking through the news-room to his office. "He's right in there," the secretary said. He was a tall, thin man who seemed more than annoyed at having to leave his desk to escort two kids into the newsroom.

Nnamdi had never seen so many computers and desks squeezed into such a small space. The fluorescent lights were tinted an ugly yellow and there was only one window, which was near the ceiling.

"Ugh, this place smells like dirty socks," Chioma whispered.

Nnamdi didn't know what he'd expected, but it wasn't this cramped newsroom. Not from a uniquely successful newsletter that thrived on embellished overblown stories and . . . murder. He knocked on the closed door on the other side of the newsroom that said, *Ikenne Kenkwo, Editor in Chief.*

"No changing into the Man," Chioma quickly said. "Let's handle this ourselves. You and me."

"Yeah, yeah," Nnamdi muttered. But he could feel the Man wanting to come forward.

"Enter, it's open," a voice said. Nnamdi pushed the door open and was bathed in sunshine. The walls here were a stunning white. The shelves were made of dark oak wood and topped with colored books and trophies. A PhD in microbiology was framed and hung in the center of the wall. The desk was expensive-looking, like the Chief of Chiefs' desk in his home office, and the computer had a large flat-screen.

The newsletter's editor in chief, Ikenne Kenkwo, wore a white dress shirt with a red tie, and his mustache was so perfectly trimmed that it didn't look real. He grinned at them and said, "It's so good to see kids taking interest in the wonderful art of—" The grin dropped from his face when he noticed Nnamdi.

"Yes, it's me. Police Chief Icheteka's son. Chioma, shut the door," Nnamdi coolly said.

"Nnamdi," Chioma said quietly.

"Just do it," Nnamdi snapped. He clenched his fists as he felt a powerful urge to change into the Man. As Nnamdi held the Man back, he noticed that his vision had a slightly red tinge. It was so slight that he wouldn't have noticed if it weren't for the white walls of the office. "We came here to face him, right?"

Chioma nodded.

Nnamdi smirked when he heard the door shut. "Good," he said.

Kenkwo was eyeing him closely now. "I can call security," Kenkwo said. "But I'd only do that if I were afraid." He leaned back in his luxuriant chair. "What do you want?"

"What do you think I want?" Nnamdi asked.

"I think you want something from me that you cannot get," he said. "Once a story is printed, it cannot be taken back. The public has seen it. It is immortal."

"I'm not here for some stupid story you printed about me." The red tinge in his eyesight grew a bit redder. Nnamdi clenched his fists again; he wanted to change so badly. This man deserved to be terrified.

They stared at each other for a long time. Nnamdi could

hear Chioma fidgeting behind him. He didn't blame her for being nervous. He was doing everything in his power *not* to change into the Man, but he was slowly slipping and the more he strained and tried to contain his anger, the redder things grew. His instincts heightened. He could almost smell the guilt coming off Kenkwo. The part of him that was the Man wanted to change and tear him apart. The part of him that was Nnamdi wanted to sit down and cry and cry. This was the man who'd robbed his father of life, made his mother a widow, who'd taken one of the two people he most loved in the world. Who had caused so much sorrow in his family. Who had done injustice to Kaleria. It was so sad and infuriating.

"I want you to admit that you killed my father," Nnamdi flatly said. His throat felt dry and his stomach queasy.

Kenkwo scoffed. "You're crazy," he said. "I'm calling security. I want you out of my office right now." He picked up the phone.

That was it for Nnamdi. He let go. It was like inhaling fresh air after holding his breath for two minutes. The red in his eyesight cleared. He felt himself rise several feet as he grew from five feet to seven. He could *hear* Kenkwo's eyes widen, the skin stretching and the tears sucking at his eyeballs. The sound of Kenkwo dropping the phone was so clear that Nnamdi could hear the tiny crack that snaked up the side of the earpiece.

Kenkwo whimpered.

"You scream and it'll be the last sound to come out of your mouth," Nnamdi said, his voice deep and sonorous. He leaned a shadowy hand on Kenkwo's expensive oak desk. Then he pushed down until he heard it start to crack. "Did you kill my father?!"

"Nnamdi, don't hurt him," Chioma whispered.

Nnamdi didn't know whether he would hurt Kenkwo or not. That was up to Kenkwo. Still, he was aware of Chioma just behind him, and he let that knowledge keep him steady.

Kenkwo's mouth flapped as he tried to speak. "W . . . w . . . witchcraft! E-e-vil juju. God help me!" he whimpered.

Nnamdi wanted to slap Kenkwo's shocked face. He reached forward and grabbed him by the collar and then pulled him over the desk. He held Kenkwo up to his shadowy face. "Did you kill my father?" Nnamdi hissed. His heightened senses picked up Kenkwo's rapid heartbeat, his overpowering expensive cologne, and the scent of adrenaline wafting from his pores. Lastly, he realized that the man wasn't breathing. Nnamdi shoved him back. "Stop holding your breath! BREATHE!!"

Kenkwo's mouth still hung open, but finally he blinked and began to inhale, his nostrils flaring and tears rolling down his cheeks. Nnamdi looked at him in disgust. He was about to grab him again when Kenkwo spoke. "I did," he said in a small, small voice. "Now the Lord has sent the devil to kill me, o."

Behind him, Chioma gasped.

Nnamdi leaned forward. "*What* did you say?"

"I . . . I sh-sh-shot your father," he said, tears dropping from his eyes. "I didn't know what else to do. The newsletter was going under. It has been in my family for generations. This paper survived colonialism, even the Biafran Civil War! For it to fold now, during a time of peace? Just because of the internet? I would be such a failure!"

"So to save your newsletter, you killed my father?! Just so you could have more negative stories to report?"

"I . . . I was desperate! And after that happened, look at the turnaround this place made! We're going to move into a new building. . . ."

"And the letter?" Nnamdi asked, his chest tight and his deep voice thick.

"That was me, too. I had a boy deliver it. The boy had nothing to do with it."

Nnamdi felt a sob wanting to escape his chest. His hands shook, hungry for Kenkwo's soft murdering neck. He would squeeze and squeeze until Kenkwo was dead.

"Nnamdi," Chioma said.

But Nnamdi couldn't speak. He didn't want to speak. He wanted to act. Chioma suddenly stepped up beside him. "You will confess then!" she shouted. Nnamdi slowly looked down at Chioma and met her eyes. She looked back at Kenkwo and quickly continued, "Write it all on paper, sign it, and then go straight to the police and confess!"

Nnamdi stared at her, feeling his entire body tingle. Chioma was . . . Chioma was right.

"*You will write your confession here,*" he roared at Kenkwo in his angriest voice, throwing the notebook and pen at him. "*You will immediately give it to your assistant editor. Then you will go straight to the police department and turn yourself in.*" He leaned on the desk again. "AND IF YOU DON'T . . ." He raised his fist and smashed it down on the desk. It buckled in two with a satisfying crunch.

Kenkwo nodded, still in his expensive leather chair, limp with fear.

Nnamdi felt himself coil as tight as a spring. Then . . . then he just let go. He had the truth. It was over. He relaxed and when he did, he changed back. He looked at Chioma.

"Okay?" she asked.

"Yes." He turned to Kenkwo. "Do we have an understanding?"

"We do," Kenkwo whispered, staring at Nnamdi. Then he hung his head. "We do."

Nnamdi wrinkled his nose. Kenkwo had peed in his pants. Good.

That day, two kids left the *Kaleria Sun*, taking with them the greatest story in Kaleria's history.

Pride

NNAMDI WOKE EARLY the next morning and quickly dressed. He was at the door when his mother came out of her bedroom.

"Where are you going? And why are you up so early?"

"I just want to buy a newsletter before I get ready for school," he said.

He hadn't told his mother a thing. How could he? His mother was happy and he didn't want to ruin that for anything. He ran out into the early morning. The sun hadn't risen yet and people were outside washing their cars and motorbikes, buying akara and bread for breakfast, leaving for work.

There was already a line in front of the newsletter stand. Nnamdi stood behind a tall, regal woman who looked like she worked for the president. Her phone went off, but she only brought it out, silenced it, and put it back in her purse. Everyone was oddly quiet. Those who got their copies slowly walked away, their eyes glued to the front page.

After a few minutes, the woman in front of him noticed Nnamdi behind her. "Oh!" she said. "Nnamdi!"

"Yes?" Nnamdi said. He didn't know the woman.

"I buy tomatoes from your mother's stall. She and I went to school together," she said. She put an arm around Nnamdi's shoulders and moved him forward. "People, let him go to the front!" she said. "This is Chief Icheteka's son!"

Everyone in line turned around and Nnamdi felt his face grow heated.

"Go on," the woman said, gently pushing him forward. As Nnamdi slowly walked to the front of the line, people occasionally patted his shoulder. "Sorry, o," some said. It was like a strange dream. The sun had just come up and all eyes were on him. He had to work to move his legs. He didn't like the looks on people's faces. They reminded him of the way people had looked at him for weeks after his father was shot. The newsletter seller gently placed a newsletter in his hands. He looked down at it.

"Editor in Chief Confesses to the Murder of Chief of Police Egbuche Icheteka," the headline read. Nnamdi suddenly felt unsteady on his feet, but he didn't stumble or sit down. He stood tall and proud. The newsletter reported that its own editor in chief was a "megalomaniac nutcase" who would rather see Kaleria writhing with crime he could report than clean and quiet.

"I'm sorry for your loss," a man said, patting him on the

shoulder as he read. "At least they finally got the killer."

"Thanks," he said, and quickly headed home.

Mr. Oke was sitting at his station near the gate when Nnamdi returned.

"Good morning," he said, smiling too big. Then he saw the newsletter in Nnamdi's hand and dropped the smile from his face. "You saw."

Nnamdi nodded.

Mr. Oke came and gave him a tight hug. "Don't look like that," he said. "It's good that they caught him."

"I know," Nnamdi said. He let go of Mr. Oke. "It's just . . . It feels like it's happening all over again."

Mr. Oke shook his head sadly. "That kind of thing only happens once."

"Yeah," Nnamdi said.

"Does your mother know?"

"She didn't when I left the house."

Nnamdi looked away from Mr. Oke's concerned face and slowly walked inside.

"Mommy," Nnamdi called. When there was no response, he went to her bedroom. She wasn't there. He looked in the bathroom, the living room, calling and calling. No response. He finally found her in the garden, staring at the yam. The healthy plant had started to grow a new tuber in the last week. Her phone was in her hand and her head was to her chest.

"Mommy, did you . . ."

"Bonny just told me," she said, looking up with dry, twitchy eyes. "That *evil* editor. The man is sick!" She covered her face with her hand and sighed a long, sad sigh. All Nnamdi could do was wrap his arms around her. His small arms. Eventually, his mother took Nnamdi's newsletter and read the entire article.

Then Nnamdi got ready for school and his mother got ready for work. Life went on.

Darling was still at large. The Chief of Chiefs was still running things with a soft hand. But when he thought about it, Nnamdi had to admit, the streets of Kaleria were quieter. And he also had to admit that a large part of this was because of him; Bad Market and Never Die were in jail and Three Days' Journey's car ring was broken. As he walked to school with Chioma, Nnamdi felt good. For now this was enough.

"Nnamdi," Ruff Diamond said, joining them. "We heard."

"Oh yeah?" Nnamdi asked.

"Yeah," Ruff Diamond said.

He winked at Nnamdi and Nnamdi smirked and looked away.

"Glad they caught him," Hassan said, joining them. "Finally."

"He turned himself in," Nnamdi said.

"That's not what my uncle says," Ruff Diamond said,

grinning. "He's a reporter at the *Kaleria Sun*, and he says the Man paid him a visit." He winked at Nnamdi again and Nnamdi's skin prickled.

"He actually *saw* the Man?" Chioma asked, catching Nnamdi's eye.

"No, he wasn't there," Ruff Diamond said. "It's just what people are guessing, I guess." He grinned. "And it makes sense to me."

Jide joined them, too. Soon the conversation turned from the confession of Nnamdi's father's murderer to the subject of Darling and how attractive she was. Chioma groaned and plugged her fingers in her ears and they all laughed.

Nnamdi woke in the middle of the night to the sound of scratching. His eye immediately went to the X-Men pencil case with the Ikenga inside it. He could see the Ikenga glowing red through the sides of the case and its machete was poking and cutting tears in it. He bolted up, barely awake. But his mind was clear. He listened for voices in his head. Was someone being attacked? His Ikenga had never glowed before and the only time it had moved was when Chioma had held it on that first night.

He slipped his shoes on and climbed out his window in his pajamas.

On instinct, he walked out of the gate. He saw his father's

ghost before he even got to the streetlight. Nnamdi could see right through him. He didn't look nearly as substantial as he had the first time. He wore his police uniform, the green beret perfectly perched atop his head. He was smiling.

"Nnamdi," his father said.

"So much has happened, Daddy."

His father nodded. "I know. And I am so proud of you, Nnamdi."

Nnamdi grinned, but in his heart there was sadness.

"This is the last time I will be able to speak to you like this," his father said.

"I know," Nnamdi said.

"I'm ashamed that my gift turned out to be a sort of curse to you," he said. "I was selfish. You're my son. You need to choose your own path. I shouldn't have tried to force mine on you."

"No, Daddy. I mean, yes, at first, it was a curse, but . . . I learned so much about the importance of responsibility, choices, controlling myself, and that things may not always be what they seem. Not to mention having smart friends like Chioma. I am glad you gave me the Ikenga."

His father smiled sadly and nodded. "Come walk with me."

As they walked, a cool fog rolled in and Nnamdi could not see the homes or the trees or the few people on the streets at this late hour. In his own words, Nnamdi told him the whole story—about Three Days' Journey, Mama Go-Slow, the abandoned school, the mango- and crime-filled town of Tse-Kucha, Never Die, the Chief of Chiefs, everything. His father laughed hard and requested silly details, like the look on Mama Go-Slow's face when Nnamdi shoved her in that car. The more he asked Nnamdi to recall, the more Nnamdi laughed, too.

"So *you* tell *me* about the Chief of Chiefs," Nnamdi finally said.

His father didn't answer for a moment. Then he stopped walking and looked at Nnamdi. "We were close. Good friends."

"Does Mama know?"

"No." He started walking again and Nnamdi knew that part of the conversation was over.

His father asked about his mother and he didn't appear angry when Nnamdi told him about Bonny. "He's a good man," his father said.

It was just like old times when they would sit in the kitchen and talk and talk. Nevertheless, soon, their conversation grew quiet and they just walked. Nnamdi sniffed, wiping a tear from his eye.

"Nnamdi, I don't want you to cry. . . ."

"But I can't help it."

There was more silence. Nnamdi could not touch his father. Those times were already over.

His father held up his palm. The wooden Ikenga sat in its

center. His father could touch that. "I will take this from you now," he said. "It is ours, but it is trouble."

Nnamdi pursed his lips. "Daddy, I would like to have it," he said. "I . . . I think eventually I will grow into it. And I can do so much good for Kaleria."

"So many before you have called it a burden, Nnamdimma. You don't have to—"

"No," Nnamdi insisted. "Well, it is a burden. But carrying it makes me strong . . . and wise. And that woman Darling is still out there. Daddy, I will be better. I'll be the best thing Kaleria has ever seen!"

His father cocked his head and thought about it for a moment. He handed the Ikenga back to Nnamdi. It was the only thing in the world that both Nnamdi and his father's spirit could touch. Nnamdi grasped it firmly, relishing the moment when both he and his father held it. When his father let go, he held it to his chest.

"I have to go now, Nnamdi," his father said. "Greet the Chief of Chiefs for me." With a knowing look in his eye, he added, "And keep an eye on that one, as I did. He is . . . tricky."

Nnamdi watched his father walk away. Soon his father's spirit vanished into the fog. Nnamdi watched the empty space for a moment, then put the Ikenga in his pocket and went home.

❧ ❧ ❧ ❧

Nnamdi stopped at his garden. It was flooded in moonlight, in serenity, peace, and quiet. He looked at the garden with the eyes of the boy he knew he still was. He exhaled as he took in every little detail in the moonlight. Chioma's sunflowers were nearly two feet high and growing. She said she'd put some kind of fast-growing plant food in them. A small blue moth landed on one of the green shoots. Nnamdi smiled. His yam had sprouted another two vines. The tomatoes, peppers, onions, and cucumbers were doing wonderfully. And the mango tree was heavy with soon-to-ripen fruits. All was well here. Again.

ACKNOWLEDGMENTS

I STARTED WRITING *Ikenga* back in 2010, so this novel was a long time coming. *Ikenga* was born from decades of visits to Imo State, Nigeria. Particularly the towns and villages of Owerri, Arondizuogu (where my father is from), and Isiekenesi (where my mother is from). These places had a different rhythm and soul than Nigeria's most known mega-city, Lagos. And in these places, there were ikenga.

I'd like to thank Nollywood director Tchidi Chikere, with whom I worked closely on the early versions of this book. Tchidi helped me find Nnamdi's voice and drive and the heart of Kaleria. Many thanks to Bibi Bakare-Yusuf, co-founder and publishing director of one of Africa's leading publishing houses, Cassava Republic, and the Cassava Republic team for all the polishing and polishing and POLISHING. It was all so worth it. To my editor Regina Hayes for her keen eye. And many thanks to my daughter Anyango, who was the first reader of this manuscript so many years ago. She loved it and that meant the world to me.